IT HAPPENED IN ALICEVILLE

IT HAPPENED IN ALICEVILLE

J. F. BRINDLEY

PALMETTO
P U B L I S H I N G
Charleston, SC
www.PalmettoPublishing.com

Copyright © 2024 by J. F. Brindley

All rights reserved

No portion of this book may be reproduced, stored in a retrieval system, or transmitted in any form by any means—electronic, mechanical, photocopy, recording, or other—except for brief quotations in printed reviews, without prior permission of the author.

Paperback ISBN: 979-8-8229-4760-3

THE ACKNOWLEDGEMENT

This novel was only possible for me to write with the help of Ruth Beaumont Cook's book "Guests Beyond the Barbed Wire" and Dr. Linda Thompson's vast medical knowledge.

Mrs. Cook's historical knowledge of the German Prison Camp makes the events that occurred there fascinating and worthy of remembering. Dr. Thompson filled me in on medicine and medical procedures common to the 1940's.

DEDICATION

This book is dedicated to Ruth Basinger, Becky Sullivan and Elizabeth Patterson. They were amazingly instrumental in writing and editing this story. We hope you enjoy it.

CHAPTER 1

MARCH 1942

The German U-boat left the North Atlantic where it had been patrolling and headed toward the coast off Racife, Brazil. The captain had timed his arrival to be at sundown. He had not submerged until he was within ten miles of the coast because he could keep a much higher speed on the surface than when the boat was submerged. Now, he went to radio silence to increase his chances of not being identified. He had been in these waters two years before, but this time he knew he was beginning a much more important and dangerous mission. He raised the sub to periscope depth and set a course north/ northwest. He followed the shoreline staying less than five miles offshore into the Caribbean Sea. He knew the Americans were certainly not expecting a U-boat to come this close to their gulf shore so soon after war had been declared. He had been briefed before leaving his home port of Hamburg that the American navy had begun building a base at Recife, Brazil, which was the most eastern point of land on the South American continent. It was not operational yet, but the opportunity to use these waters as a way to gain access to the United States would never be as readily available in the future as it was now. The captain knew continuation of the radio silence was essential for his success, and his crew, even the cooks, made every effort to prevent any noise from breaking the silence.

The night slowly passed and at midmorning the captain raised the periscope to see if there was any activity along the Central America coast after the sub had bypassed ships approaching the Panama Canal. He did see several fishing boats headed west toward the coast, but nothing else except a few sea gulls. The radio operator had begun picking up Mexican music and commentators broadcasting the news and the weather in Spanish. After passing the Yucatan peninsula there was a lack of any significant development that could be seen from the sub. The captain looked at his watch and after about twenty minutes signaled to turn the sub to the east. The engine speed was greatly reduced, and the sub crawled slowly eastward the rest of the day. After sundown the sub engine came to a complete stop. A sailor went to the wardroom and told the two male passengers to report to the captain.

The passengers were both dressed in khaki pants, cotton shirts and baseball caps, and both carried a seabag. The captain was waiting for them and spoke softly as they approached him. "We have arrived at the drop off point. The weather is clear; the sea is quite calm, and your dingy will be easy to maneuver. Check your compass and travel directly north. I expect you to be safely on land before daylight."

Both men nodded and moved to the ladder leading to the top of the sub. The sub was slowly rising now, and when the captain lowered the periscope, he signaled to his crew. Several began moving up the ladder. The leader opened the hatch and they all climbed out. The moon was shining brightly, and all could see that the sea was calm. The two passengers were signaled to follow the men up the ladder. The captain led the final group who brought up the dingy and after inflating it, slipped it into the water. The passengers handed their seabags to the nearest crew member and watched them being carefully placed in the dingy.

Turning to the captain, both passengers shook his hand and one said, "Thank you for our safe arrival. We will meet again after the war and recall our time together."

The captain nodded and smiled. He watched the two carefully move over the side of the sub and get seated in the dingy, wave to the crew, and began paddling away. When they were significantly far enough away, the captain and crew members disappeared back inside the sub and closed the hatch. The sub slowly submerged and retraced its way back to the Atlantic.

'The two Germans continued paddling north looking for land. When the sky began to grow lighter, they began paddling faster. Finally, they had gotten close enough to the shoreline to see that it looked completely deserted. When the water became shallow enough, they stepped out of the dingy and pulled it ashore. They walked up the beach carrying their seabags and dragging the dingy. They climbed over a sand dune and used a pocketknife to deflate the little rubber boat rapidly. Using their hands, they dug into the sand to bury it. When they were satisfied that the dingy was completely hidden, they continued walking away from the coast until they came to a road. Soon they heard a vehicle and they both put up their thumbs. The car didn't stop, so they resumed walking. When they heard another vehicle, they again stopped and put up their thumbs. A pickup truck stopped, and a teenage boy rolled down his window and said, "I'm going to Panama City if you all would like a ride."

"Great, we are going there too. We left our jobs in New Jersey before Christmas and have been touring the south. Now we are both looking for jobs," answered the nearest man.

The teenager laughed and said, "I hear the army is hiring!"

The second man said, "Yes, I heard that too, but they do not want us. I'm color blind and my brother here has asthma. Actually, we are hoping to open a photography shop. Is Panama City a good place for a photography shop?"

"Are you kidding! PC has the most beautiful beaches in the world. Just wait until you see the white sand beach. Climb up in the back and hang on. We will be there very shortly," the teen said.

Both men threw their sea bags in the truck, climbed in and sat down on them as the truck began to move. They smiled at each other. Their English had been acceptable. They were in the United States!

The two German spies had arrived in Florida and were ready to begin their mission.

CHAPTER 2

APRIL 1942

Norma Fleming used two bobby pins to secure her nurse's cap in place. She glanced at the mirror over her dresser, grabbed her purse, and headed for the door to her apartment. She had just touched the doorknob when she heard the phone ring. She turned back into the living room and hurried to the hall to answer the phone that sat in its inset.

"Hello," she answered, wondering who would be calling her this early in the morning.

"Sis, I am so glad I caught you before you left for work. I have made a decision and wanted you to be the first to know. I am going to join the army as soon as we hang up. Several of my buddies have already joined. I have only hesitated because of mom and dad, but I decided you will just have to come home and help them until this war is over. Hopefully, it will not be too long," said her brother Ben.

"This is certainly a surprise. I know how much you love Aliceville. I can't imagine mom and dad are happy with your decision."

"I have not told them, but you know they would only try to talk me out of it. I can't just sit here and let others do my fighting for me. You know the U.S. finished the Great War pretty quickly after they had been fighting for years in Europe," Ben answered.

"Oh Ben, I am having a tough time getting my thoughts together. Will you just hold your horses until I have a chance to think this through? I just can't up and leave my job without giving any notice and would have to move out of my apartment. I don't see how I could leave in less than a month. I'm not even sure if my car will make the trip from here to Aliceville," Norma said.

"Sis, don't you remember I came up to Nashville to see Alabama and Vanderbilt play football two years ago? It wasn't that far. If you don't think your car will make the trip, just sell your car and come on the train. You certainly don't need a car to get around Aliceville, Pickens County, Alabama! If you need to go to Carrollton or Tuscaloosa, you can always use dad's truck," Ben replied.

"If you leave right now, I won't even get to see you. Please put off enlisting until I can get home," Norma pleaded.

"Sorry, Norma, but I've made up my mind. You remember Mr. Carter. He is driving to Carrollton this morning and will take me there where a recruiter is waiting. I am leaving the business office now and going out onto the main floor to tell dad I am leaving. I kissed mom this morning before I left the house but will have to let dad tell her when he goes home for lunch. I couldn't deal with her crying and all. So, don't you start crying on the telephone."

"Ben, I do so love you. I am not crying, but I am tearing up. Please take care of yourself and write to me from wherever the army sends you for training," she said.

"Bye Sis," he said and hung up the phone. He looked out the window of the office and saw his dad sweeping the floor of the hardware store before he unlocked the front door and hung up the open sign. Ben took a deep breath and headed to his father.

In Nashville, Norma hung up her phone and began crying. She genuinely loved her brother and knew she regretted that he was joining the army, but at the same time she was very proud of him. She wiped her face with a tissue from her purse and headed for the front door to face a day quite different from what she had expected less than five minutes ago.

By the time she reached Vanderbilt Hospital, she had sketched out a plan on how to leave this job and city she had grown to love in the six years she had lived here. She would immediately tell her supervisor she was having to leave and begin the process of resigning. At her first break this morning, she would call her boyfriend and ask him to meet her for lunch where she would have to break the news to him. Neither of these things were going to be pleasant or easy. Her anger with the Japanese and the Germans had just gotten very personal!

CHAPTER 3

MAY 1942

The two German spies had been busy the few weeks they had been in Panama City, Florida. First, they had found a motel near the main part of the city and got settled in. Then they walked around to become familiar with their surroundings. Next, they had opened a joint checking account and deposited $20,00 American dollars in a local bank. They are using the names that were on the fake drivers' licenses, supposedly issued from New Jersey, which they had brought from Germany. Now they were John and James Webb instead of Otto Webber and Hanes Muller.

They had searched the daily newspaper until they found a house only a few blocks away for rent and had signed a lease for a year. They had used the $20,00 to transform the old house into a photography shop. As you entered the living room it held a counter with a cash register. A sign-in roster was available as were several comfortable chairs. On one side wall a showcase held cameras and special lenses. Behind it were shelves with all different kinds of film. Across the hall the dining room had two cameras set up on tripods with several different back drops affixed to the walls. Lights and large open white umbrellas were behind stools and benches where customers could be seated. There were several baskets filled with toys to entertain children.

John and James each had a bedroom. The third bedroom had become a storage area, and the one bathroom would be shared by the men and would be available for customers. The kitchen was transformed into their dark room with blackout curtains.

The refrigerator had been moved into the garage as well as a card table and two folding chairs. The plan was to eat cold cereal for breakfast and make sandwiches for lunch here in the garage. Their dinner would be in bars or cafes so they could meet people and learn more about the area as well as learn about places to visit where pictures could be taken of potential targets for German aircraft. There was still room in the garage for the 1936 Plymouth they had bought from an old man who was moving in with his son. The Plymouth needed work, but James had been a mechanic and knew he could do any work that the car needed. Both men knew that gasoline would be very difficult to buy, but they knew they could not do their jobs without being able to travel. They had been given a name, a password, and address in New Orleans where they were to deliver pictures and any other useful information every few months. This trip to New Orleans was going to be one of the many problems they were facing.

Finally, on the last day of the month, they had placed an advertisement in the local newspaper to run for a week. Today they stood in their front yard looking at their sign that read: Webb Cameras and Photography, Come in and shop from 9 to 5, Monday thru Friday.

They spent the rest of the day going over everything they had accomplished in the few weeks they had been in the city. They could not afford any slip ups because they were down to their last $50. When both were satisfied, they relaxed and read their orders for the last time before burning them in the back yard. The following Monday morning John and James stood behind the counter in their own business awaiting their first customer.

It was a little past 10 am when a young girl came in. She approached the counter and before she could speak James said, "Good morning, how can I help you?"

She smiled and said, "I want to have my picture taken for my boyfriend. He is leaving-for the summer and asked me

> for a picture to take with him. I was wondering how much it would cost to have a real professional picture made?"

"Since you are our very first customer, I will give you a special, one time only price. How does $5.00 sound? Especially, if we could keep a copy to display here in our shop," James answered

"I guess that would be okay. I have never had a picture taken in a studio before. Can you do it now?"

> "Yes, I can. Let's have you sign this contract and then move you over to a seat right in front of the camera and get you set up," James smiled as he moved from behind the counter, led the young girl across the room to where the picture would be taken and indicated where she should sit.

"I will take several different shots and you can stop back by on Thursday and pick out the pose you like best. Then you can decide on the size and how many copies you would like. Of course, if you order more than one there will be an additional cost," James explained.

Before she left, a second customer came in and John stepped up to help her. She asked about buying film for her camera. John got it from a shelf behind the showcase and sold it to her.

A steady flow of customers passed through the shop all day long. Webb Photography was up and running. The money they had brought from Germany had been enough to get them settled in their new business. By its second month it was showing a profit. It operated for the next three years.

CHAPTER 4

MAY 1942

It had taken Norma longer than she expected to quit her job, pack her clothes and a few items she wanted to keep, dispose of the furniture she had bought mostly at secondhand stores, say goodbye to her friends, and drive out of Nashville. On her trip home, she relived her last six years. She had come to Nashville right after high school to attend nursing school at Vanderbilt University. Her grandfather had left her a substantial amount of money in his will, and this money paid for her training. Her good grades meant she was offered a job following her graduation at Vanderbilt Hospital which she had immediately snapped up. She, of course, had been back home to Aliceville to visit with her family and friends occasionally in the following years, but had not expected to return home to live.

Now, she was driving back home, without any hope of working in a hospital because Aliceville didn't have a hospital! The only doctors' offices in town stayed full of patients, but anyone who needed surgery or was too sick to return home was treated in Carrolton or Tuscaloosa. Since she was returning home to provide support for her parents with their hardware store and their farm, there was no way she could drive to either city to work.

She remembered her brother, Ben, had not gone to college after graduation from high school, but had gone to work full-time in their father's hardware store. The store was a successful business, and it needed him to slowly replace his father, who was no longer capable of operating as salesclerk, manager and owner. Norma could not see herself working in a hardware store. She had no remembrance of ever selling anything in the store or even opening the cash register. At least she could keep the books for the business and perhaps make the orders for new merchandise.

As for the farm, her dad had a man and his wife living there now, Wilma and Milton Bowen. They did the farm work and cared for the farm animals. They had lost their own farm in the depression and were happy to have a nice home to live in and easy work for the Flemings. Her parents had moved to the town when her grandfather died since they inherited the hardware store and the family home. Norma's dad still loved the farm and just couldn't bring himself to sell it. Norma knew there was really no work there for her at the farm.

However, she knew her mother was diabetic and had almost crippling arthritis, and she could easily see herself caring for her and keeping house for them all. She could drive both parents anywhere they needed to go because both didn't see well, and their reaction time was not what it had been in the past. These jobs would not take up all of her time and she would need to find some way she could support the war effort.

When she finally arrived at her parents' house, it was already getting dark. She drove into the driveway and parked behind her dad's pickup. Both parents had been waiting for her and heard her car. They both met her on the front porch and Norma and her mother hugged and kissed each other. Her dad took the suitcase from her and all three went inside.

"Honey, we were getting so anxious. I told your dad that surely you would get here in time for supper, "said Norma's mother, Florence.

"I am hungry. It is good to finally be here. What have you heard from Ben? I only got one letter since he arrived at Fort Benning."

"He wrote us a letter also. I guess they are keeping him very busy. Come on to the table. Mother will be taking the food out of the oven and bringing it out," said her dad.

It wasn't long after supper until they all went upstairs to bed. Norma went into her old room and was always amused that it had not changed in any way since she had originally left it. She changed into her pajamas and climbed into bed. She wrote a letter to Frank, her boyfriend, before she turned out the light. She could still see him standing on the street throwing her a kiss as she pulled the car from the parking place in front of her apartment building. Norma knew this separation was going to be very hard for both of them.

It had been a long day and she was very tired. Within a few short minutes she was asleep. Sometime during the night, she dreamed she was back in nursing school and was very homesick. When she woke up, she realized it was a dream and she certainly was not in school and certainly not homesick for Aliceville! If anything, she was already homesick for Nashville and her fiancé Dr. Frank Williams. He was her dentist the third year she lived in Nashville, and after meeting him, they began dating and had just gotten engaged.

CHAPTER 5

When Norma came downstairs the following morning, her parents were already at the breakfast table. Her mother smiled and said, "Oh, I expected you to sleep in this morning. Your dad has to be up to go open the store now that Ben is away."

"I can do that dad, if you trust me," said Norma.

"Of course, I trust you, but let me do it today. I will give you a few instructions before you get to open up. Why not come over later this morning so we can walk through the details before you get the full monte thrust upon you."

"What is the full monte?" asked Norma.

"Your dad has a shortwave radio in his office at the store. He listens to the British broadcasting to their many nations, and he has heard them refer to Field Marshall Montgomery who appears to be quite long winded by that term. It has become a part of his everyday speech. Now George, go on to work. I plan on a long talk with my daughter before I send her to that old store and all of those old friends of yours who hang around there," her mother said.

"You hear that, Norma? Now you know who the boss is around here," her dad said as he smiled and got up from the table, put on his old straw hat and headed for the door.

"Ben and I always knew who the boss was Dad. Some things never change. I'll be over later on this morning after I have some of this good smelling breakfast and a talk with my mother."

He nodded his head and left. Norma dove into the biscuits and gravy and began eating. Her mother had poured her a big mug of coffee and began clearing the dirty plates and silverware off the table. "Take all the time you want eating. I just want to get these dishes cleared away so we can visit," she said.

"Mom, nobody makes better gravy. I am going to have to remember that I don't want to be as big as the house from eating your good cooking! Is there something special you want to talk about, or should we just gossip about Aliceville?"

"Well, I guess I want to ask you about coming home. I know you told me the last time you were home that you loved your job and Nashville. You also mentioned that one man you were dating. I don't want you to change your life because of your dad and me. I know you told me on the phone that you wanted to come and be with us, but I wanted to see your face when you said that."

"Mom, please accept that I needed to come home and am here because it is where I should be. Ben knew that when he called me to come. The war will be changing everyone's life. Yes, I did, no do love Nashville, but I also love Aliceville and my family.

"I know you love us, but Vanderbilt Hospital is a very good hospital. I was so proud to say you were working there, and how about that man you were dating. Is he out of the picture?"

"No. Frank and I are still a couple. I believe he will be giving me a diamond for my birthday. I really like his mother and father, and I think he told them that he would be coming here with me the very first time both of us were off from work together. I actually have already invited him to come here as soon as he can get away. I do want you and dad to meet him."

"That is wonderful. Of course, he will be very welcome. Is he tall, dark and handsome?"

"Yes. He actually looks a lot like dad must have looked like as a young man."

"In that case, I will certainly like him! Your father will have a hard time liking anyone who is planning on marrying his daughter, but he can be won over. Just don't tell him until he has begun to like uh......oh, what is his name again?"

"He is Dr. Frank Williams. Remember me telling you he is actually a dentist. He went to Duke as an undergrad and came to Vanderbilt for his dental training. Like me, he liked Nashville so much he decided to stay. His parents will probably move there when his father retires. They currently live near Knoxville. I met them when they came to visit Frank and his sister who also lives in Nashville.

"I think that means you will be living in Nashville after you get married. I am so sorry you feel an obligation to be here until Ben gets back home. Your dad and I don't think we need a babysitter just because we are not spring chickens. Is there any way that you can get your job back if you return to Nashville?"

"Mom, I gave up my apartment and there was already a waiting list of people who needed a place to live. NO, I am not returning to Nashville."

"I didn't mean now, I meant after the war and you get married," explained her mom.

"That will be some time much later and who knows what conditions will have changed by then. Now, I think I would want to go back and work at Vanderbilt, but we will just have to wait and see," Norma said.

Their conversation turned to other things and continued for almost an hour before the phone rang. Norma got up and went to the phone attached to the wall and after saying hello she heard, "Norma, I would know that voice anywhere. This is Connie. Your mother told me you would get home last night. I just couldn't wait any longer to call you. This is my planning time and I hoped you were still there. Can you come to my house for dinner tonight? I can hardly believe you are home to stay."

Norma was laughing when she answered. "I would love to come and eat with you. I am leaving now to go to the store to learn whatever Dad thinks I have to know to work there, and then I will be back here to unpack and settle in. What time shall I come?"

"I get home from school by 3:45, so as soon as possible after that. I want to catch up on all you have been up to, and I want to tell you all that is going on in my life. I have to go to class now before those 4th graders tear up my room. See you this afternoon. Bye now," Connie answered.

Norma turned away from the telephone and said, "Connie invited me to her house for dinner. When I get back from seeing dad, I can do anything here you would like before I go there. "

"I am so glad she called you. When I saw her in church, I told her you were coming home. She was so excited. You girls were almost joined at the hip all the way through school. I don't think you ever were cross with each other. Go on now and visit with your dad. He will think you aren't coming if you don't go now. Anyway, you can walk back with him for lunch," Norma's mom said.

After spending time with her dad at the hardware store, walking home with him for lunch, and unpacking her clothes, Norma kissed her mother and left for her friend Connie's home. She arrived at 4:30 pm and was greeted by Connie and her young son, Tony.

"It is just wonderful that you are going to be here for a while. Can you see how much Tony has grown since you were here last Christmas? Say hello to Aunt Norma, Tony."

Tony looked down at the floor and said, "Hello, Aunt Norma."

"It's very nice to see you and your mommy, Tony. You may not remember me, but I remember you. Will you be three on your birthday?"

He nodded his head without looking up, and Connie said, "He is always shy around people he doesn't know just like his father. Come into the living room and sit down. The roast is in the oven and will take about two hours to cook so we have plenty of time to talk."

"Connie, I can see that you are expecting again. When will the newest member of your family be born?"

"The doctor gave me September 15th as the due date. That is a couple of weeks after school starts which means I will need a substitute for the first month of school. The principal has been very kind about my failing to plan this pregnancy so that the baby would be born during the summer."

"I think it is wonderful that your children are going to be so close in age. The five years between me and Ben meant we love each other but were not close when we were growing up."

"If this baby isn't a girl, I will be the mother of two boys because we just can't afford a third child. Larry is making fairly good money as a bank teller, but my teacher's salary is really keeping us afloat. I am so glad that my dad helped me by paying my tuition for my college, but you know all of that history. I want to hear about your Frank."

"We have been seriously dating for about two years now. This past year has been very special because Frank has finished all his schooling and gotten established in his practice. We have begun talking about our getting married. However, this war, and my having to come home to help mom and dad while Ben is gone, has meant that all we were planning is now on hold. I expect he will take a few days off within the next month and come down to visit. He wants to meet my folks, and I want him to meet my friends here, especially you and Larry."

"I look forward to meeting him and I am sure Larry will as well. Speaking of Larry, I just heard him pulling into the garage. I stopped at the bank on the way home from school and told him you were coming for supper. He was delighted that you were coming. Here he is now."

Larry came into the living room from the kitchen and hurried to Norma and hugged her. "Hey lady, we are so glad you are home for a while at least. I was afraid you had outgrown our little town and we would not ever see you but on holidays."

"Thank-you Larry. It is good to be here for a while. Ben was insistent that I come to be here while he is gone to the war. I already see how fragile my parents have both become in just the few months since I was here for Christmas. Ben is confident we will win this war fairly quickly and he will be back here."

"I hope he is right, but I am hearing talk about it being longer than the Great War. As a matter of fact, would you believe that two members of congress came into the bank this afternoon and I overheard them talking to my boss about plans to build a prison camp right here in Aliceville. Both men are pretty influential members of congress. They have convinced the State Department and Pentagon to build a facility right here. I think they will begin construction sometime in August."

"Are you serious? I am not sure I want a prison camp here," said Connie.

"It will bring a lot of money into our area, Connie. Just think about the builders living in the area and the military that will be coming here. I have been worried that businesses might be closing because so many men would be leaving, but this will ensure that the bank will profit financially, as well as Aliceville, because of this facility being here," said Larry.

Tony began pulling on Larry's pants leg and Larry reached down and picked him up. He kissed the boy's cheek and said, "Norma, see how this little guy is growing. He is going to be a great ball player right here at the high school."

"I am sure he will be. You used to hit those home runs every time you played. I remember sitting in the stands with Connie and cheering for you," Norma said.

This began several hours of remembering back to their high school days and didn't end until supper was ended, and the dishes were done. While Larry took Tony upstairs and got him ready for bed, Norma said goodnight to Connie and returned home. Her parents had already gone to bed and Norma quietly climbed the stairs to her room. She knew that tomorrow she would have to tell her parents what Larry Gardner had told her about the prison camp coming to Aliceville.

A prison camp in Aliceville was a totally unexpected event!

CHAPTER 6

George Fleming walked downstairs at 6:30 am just as he did every morning. He was surprised to see his daughter already up and dressed. "Daddy, are you aware that the army is going to build a prison camp here in Aliceville?"

"I have heard about the government possibly building a training base here, but don't put much hope in that. Aliceville is a pretty small town with very few facilities that would support that kind of a base. Now, I haven't heard about a prison camp, but that might be a right good choice. Prisoners don't need a lot of local shopping to meet their needs. The more I think about that the more sense it makes. Who told you that?"

"Larry Gardner told me last night. He said that the building will be started right away. He said that Representatives Bankman and Sparkman were in the bank yesterday afternoon and he overheard them talking to his boss about it. You know his boss is the chairman of the Democratic Party in this district. There will be military members moving here to be in charge of the camp, who will be bringing their families. So don't believe that Aliceville will not be growing and changing. There may even be jobs for local people to work there."

Norma's mother came downstairs and entered into the conversation. "Did I hear you say a prison camp will be built here?"

"Yes, Florence. Larry Gardner told Norma last night. I heard talk about the government building something here, but it wasn't a prison camp. This quiet little town may be about to get very busy."

"Well George, let me get your breakfast quickly because I know you will be anxious to get to the store this morning to get that coffee pot ready for your friends to get there and discuss this new turn of events," she said.

Norma followed her mother into the kitchen and began helping prepare breakfast. She carefully observed that both parents seemed more alert and excited than any time since she had gotten home. Something new to think and talk about had energized them. Norma hoped that they would keep this enthusiasm for the future.

After breakfast George headed to the store and Norma decided to take her mother and drive out to the farm to visit Wilma and Milton Bowen. It was only a ten-minute drive until Norma parked in front of the farmhouse. "Look at those marigolds blooming in the front yard. Wilma always has something blooming every time I come out here," said Norma.

"She loves flowers. Sometimes she sends Milton to town with flowers for me. I bet she is out at the barn, but we can try the front door," said her mother.

Norma knocked on the door and it opened right away. Wilma saw Norma and a big smile lit up her face as she opened the door. "My goodness, I didn't expect to see you for months. Come in child and bring your mother with you. Florence, I know you are in hog heaven with this girl home."

All three ladies greeted each other with hugs and moved through the living room into the big kitchen. "Norma couldn't wait any longer to get out here to see you."

"I know she always comes to see us when she comes home, but I know she really wants to see Doll," said Wilma.

"How is my horse?" Norma asked.

"She is just pretty as a picture. You go on to the barn and see her while I make a pot of coffee and visit with your mother."

Norma didn't need any more invitations. She was out the back door and headed down the path to the barn. Doll had been Norma's horse since her sixteenth birthday, and she never came to Aliceville without coming to see her. Norma knew she was going to be here long enough this time to get to ride Doll many times like she had done when she was in high school. There were some nice things about being back home for a while.

Norma spent a long time brushing and talking to Doll. She brought some oats and fresh water into the stall and Doll leaned her head against Norma's face. Their special relationship was still strong. Norma could have spent the whole rest of the morning with Doll, but she knew her mother would want to get back home to prepare lunch, so she reluctantly walked back to the house and joined her mother and Wilma.

"My horse is as beautiful as ever. Wilma, thank you and Milton for taking such good care of her. I will be coming regularly to visit you and ride Doll."

"I'm sure glad; we sure enjoy having you visiting us. Your mom was telling me that Ben asked you to come home and stay until he gets back from the war. I don't want a long war, but having you here is like having my kids here."

"Where are your kids now? It has been a long time since I have seen Mary Jo and Milly."

"When Milly graduated from high school, they both moved to Mobile. Mary Jo got a job as a waitress in a nice restaurant and Milly is a typist in a shipping company office. They are pretty good at writing to us. I would prefer them to be working here, but you know there aren't many jobs here."

"Norma, I told Wilma about the prison camp coming here and that there may be some more development in Aliceville. Maybe some more jobs will be coming here soon."

"I'm not sure their dad would want them working in a prison camp," said Wilma.

"I expect the military will staff the camp with all the workers who are needed there, but more people moving in the area will mean more jobs in new businesses," said Norma.

"Before you leave, Florence, I want you to bring me any canning jars and lids that are at your house the next time you come out here. I need to see how many more I need to buy. It will not be long until I have to start canning. I expect food will not be as plentiful now with so many men leaving the farms to go in the army like your Ben did."

"I'm sure you are right. I'll start collecting what I have for you. Come on now Norma; we have to get home and start fixing lunch for your dad. We have sure enjoyed our visit."

"I have too. Norma anytime you can get out here to ride Doll will be fine. Bye now."

The two ladies had enjoyed being at the farm. Norma knew she would be going there every chance she got to ride Doll. Florence knew Wilma and Milton would continue to take good care of the farm and were happy doing it. It had been a very successful morning.

When George arrived for lunch, he was anxious to tell his wife and daughter all that he had learned this morning. "The prison camp is the only thing everyone in town is talking about. Most people think Japanese prisoners will be arriving soon."

"I believe they will have to build the camp before any prisoners will be coming here," Florence said.

"Mom is right. It would be putting the cart before the horse to bring the prisoners first," Norma stated.

"Always know that your mother is always right," her dad answered. "I'll go on the street and announce that no prisoners will be arriving until the prison is built, according to my wife."

"Dad, you are so funny. Mom doesn't speak with authority. She was just being logical."

"How often is our government logical? I have lived many more years than you girl and have noticed this country's leaders can sometimes make the most illogical, downright foolish choices," George said.

Now you are not thinking about President Roosevelt, George. Mr. Hoover is long gone from Washington. The country was recovering from the depression when those Japanese attacked Pearl Harbor," Florence said.

"Don't leave out that Hitler and his Nazi party," Norma added. "I had so hoped we could stay out of this war. Poor Ben and so many young men are having their lives disrupted by involving us in a war that needed to stay in Europe."

"It will be very difficult for us to fight a war on two fronts. The draft people are going to stay busy finding the best men we have and turning them into soldiers and sailors," said George. "This war may be bloody, but I know we will win it."

George was trying to end this conversation on a positive note. He didn't want his wife and daughter to worry any more about the war and Ben. He was worried enough about Ben for the rest of the family.

CHAPTER 7

AUGUST 1942

The federal government paid $29,295 to Doc and Nannie Parker for about four hundred acres of pastureland just outside of Aliceville. The government also bought four hundred acres from six other sellers whose land adjoined the Parkers' land. All of the land was bulldozed immediately with the exception of the Parker's small family home which became the camp commander's residence and remained that throughout the war years.

A construction company from Montgomery appeared and began working on the site. Any local citizen who ventured out to see what was happening at the site was told nothing by the military men they encountered there, and the construction workers from Montgomery answered that they didn't know anything about what they were building. The townspeople referred to it as "The Jap Camp."

However, by the middle of October, the editor of the Carrollton newspaper visited the camp site and met men from all over Pickens County building barracks and making the best wages of their lives. This prison camp was certainly having a very welcome impact on the entire county, not just Aliceville.

By early November, it was becoming clear that the camp would be completed before the Corps of Engineers deadline which was sometime in December. Local people began applying for jobs at the "Aliceville Internment Camp." Of course, Norma Fleming was one of them; she applied to work at the camp hospital. Her parents had strongly encouraged her, and she knew she would have plenty of time away from her new job to be available to provide any support her parents needed. She was hired and told that she would be called to come to work when the medical supplies arrived as well as the military hospital staff.

Norma hurried home to tell her parents that she had been hired. "I know how much you have missed working in a hospital. This hospital will not be very large when compared to Vanderbilt, but it will be important for this camp and our community," said Florence to her daughter.

"I had hoped to find an opportunity to support the war effort while I was here, but I certainly didn't expect it to be at a hospital. At least I will be able to keep up with the latest best practices and the latest drugs that become available," Norma said.

"What does the camp look like inside? I can see the two fences separated by an empty area and the towers where guards will be stationed on every side to view the entire camp to prevent anyone from attempting to escape, but that is all I can see from the outside," her dad said.

"Well, the main gate actually amounts to two gates. Everyone entering is checked and double checked. Each one of us coming in this morning had to sign an agreement whereby we relieved the government of all liability for any personal or property damage which might incur while we are at the camp. The form was dated today and I was told I wouldn't have to sign it again.

We then walked down what could be called Nazi Boulevard. I could see rows of barracks on both sides of the street. Then all of us went into the headquarters building and met Col F. A. Prince, the commanding officer of the camp. I really liked him, Dad. I know you will too. Then finally I got to tour the hospital. Both prisoners and the regular personnel will be treated there. I met two doctors and viewed the medicines that have already arrived. Vanderbilt Hospital is not better stocked with medicine than this hospital will be. I am ready to begin working today. Actually, I hope the prisoners arrive soon because I will not be needed until the numbers of possible patients rises."

"It sounds like it will be quite an adventure for you and the camp has been well organized and well built. Aliceville should be proud that we will be involved in the war effort of the country," her father stated.

"My goodness, I got so interested in hearing about your morning that I almost forgot. You got a call from your boyfriend while you were out," said her mother.

Norma immediately walked to the kitchen and called Frank. He had planned to come for Thanksgiving. She knew her parents would be very impressed with his pleasant personality and obvious love for their daughter. Both Norma and Frank had sent letters each week since she had been in Aliceville, but he rarely called except on the weekends. She hoped he would be telling her that he was coming for Christmas as well as Thanksgiving.

He answered on the first ring, "Hello. This is Dr. Williams."

"I wasn't expecting you to answer. Is your receptionist out today?"

"No, I was just standing here to tell her I was expecting you to call. I want to come this weekend if possible."

"Of course, Darling. You can come anytime. My parents are anxious to get to know you."

"Good, I will leave early Friday morning. My patients will have to reschedule. I'll see you Friday. Have to go now. I have a patient in the chair. Bye, Love."

Norma was not even sure he had stayed on the line long enough to hear her goodbye. She hadn't even had a chance to ask any questions or tell him the good news that she had gotten a job at the prison hospital. She was concerned about the call, but she wasn't sure why. It would be a long wait until Friday, and she could find out what was really on Frank's mind.

"Mother, Frank is coming Friday! I am so glad. I have been missing him so much. We normally see each other every day."

"Oh goodness, I will have to make a Lemon Ice box Pie and bake a ham. Is there anything he doesn't eat? Does he drink sweet tea? I better check that the silver doesn't need to be polished. "We need to air out your brother's old room for him," Florence began making plans.

"Florence don't make yourself sick worrying about Norma's young man coming. He isn't going to be looking at the house to see if you have cleaned out all the closets and washed the curtains. He is coming to see Norma," said George. "I want to meet him too. He sounds like a nice person, but I want to see for myself."

"'Don't be ridiculous! Norma wouldn't pick a man who wasn't generous and kind. I just want him to feel like he would fit right into our family. Norma has already met his family and told me they were charming."

"Mom and Dad, you are both lovely people and I know Frank will enjoy meeting you and will like Aliceville," said Norma. "Mom, just don't wear your houses shoes and apron the whole time Frank is here, and Dad please lose that old straw hat!"

CHAPTER 8

NOVEMBER 1942

Norma was sitting on the front porch waiting for Frank to arrive when her dad came walking home from the hardware store. He looked very tired, but he smiled when he saw Norma.

"I'm so glad you are here waiting for me," he said.

"Dad, I should have relieved you this afternoon," she said.

"Now, now, you have been there three days this week. Friday afternoon is always pretty quiet anyway," he answered. "I gather that boyfriend hasn't arrived yet."

"No, but I expect him any time now. I had hoped he would come long before this."

"The man has a business to run. He can't up and run down the road at a moment's notice," he replied.

"Thank you for defending him, Dad. I'll try not to complain about it taking him so many months to come to Aliceville. I have missed him so terribly and am worried about him. He really didn't sound like himself when we talked on the phone the other day."

"Oh, that explains why you are sitting here on the porch. You are missing the man but are also worried for some reason. Well, I will go on inside and leave you to sit here and wait and worry," he said.

Norma smiled and said, "Dad you are such a tease. You are very welcome to sit here with me. You knew all along I was sitting here waiting for Frank."

George sat down and pulled out a letter from his coat pocket and said, "I got a letter from your brother this morning. Read it and it will get your mind off of Frank."

Norma took the letter and began reading. Before she finished the letter, her dad spoke up, "Looks like your friend is finally here."

Norma looked up and handed the letter back to her father. She ran to the driveway and embraced Frank as he stepped from the car. They kissed and continued the embrace while beginning to whisper to each other. George rose and entered the house to tell his wife there was no need to hurry getting the supper to the table because their daughter and her boyfriend were quite busy and appeared to not be interested in eating dinner for a while.

When the two love birds finally came in, Norma formally introduced Frank to her parents. George and Florence welcomed him to their home and told him how very happy they were to finally meet him after hearing about what a wonderful man he was from their daughter. They had set the table with the good china and silverware. Florence lit the candles and George said grace. The dinner was family style and delicious. The conversation covered current events and the history of Aliceville. Florence served coffee and pie in the living room to the two men while she and Norma quickly washed the dishes and left the kitchen spotless.

"I see you are getting along very well," Florence said as she and Norma joined the men.

"Your husband was telling me all about his farming days before moving into town and taking over the hardware store," Frank said.

"Yes, he will always be a farmer at heart," said Florence. "However, he has been quite successful in his business."

"Frank has been quite successful in his business as well," said Norma.

"I actually joined an established business, but it has increased since I came which I am pleased to say," added Frank.

"Frank's partner has told me that taking Frank as his partner was the best business decision he has ever made," Norma said proudly.

"Ladies that is enough praising us! Florence, I think it is time for us to retire upstairs and let these young people talk to each other. Norma will show you the guest room, Frank. I will see you tomorrow at breakfast. Goodnight," George said as he took his wife's hand and led her to the stairs.

Both Norma and Frank watched the old couple slowly climb the stairs and then settled down on the sofa.

"You have lovely parents," Frank said.

"Thank you. They are older than your parents as you can see. They had been married quite a number of years before I was born, and they had my brother even later."

"I am glad to have this time to talk to you because I do have something quite important to tell you," Frank said seriously.

Norma sat up straight and prepared for whatever was bothering him. She had known from his voice on the telephone call a few days ago that something was upsetting him. She sat waiting but he said nothing and kept looking down. Finally, she said, "What is it? Please tell me! I can't help if I don't know what it is."

Frank finally began talking. "A couple of days before I called you, I got a call from a friend from dental school. I don't think you ever met him. His name is Carl Atkins. Anyway, he told me that another dentist friend of his had called and told him that he had joined the navy and was already on a ship somewhere in the Pacific where he was continuing to do dental work. He told Carl not to wait to be drafted into the army because having a clean bunk at night sure beat sleeping on the ground or in a fox hole. Besides, he actually has all the instruments he needs clean and ready to use," Frank said, finally looking at Norma. "I have already joined the navy and leave for San Diego on Monday."

"You did this without telling me?" How could you?"

"Norma, you decided to leave Nashville without asking me. I remember being invited for lunch and being told. I know you are shocked, but you know I am the right age, am healthy, and not married. The draft board would have been calling me soon anyway."

"This awful war is ruining our lives. Oh, Frank, I love you so much! I can't believe you are leaving so soon."

"We have tomorrow. I will have to go back to Nashville Sunday. My parents and my sister will meet me Monday morning and take care of my apartment and car while I am gone. My partner has accepted that I am leaving and assured me my job will be waiting for me when I return. Norma, you know that I love you and want to marry you, but that will have to be put off for a while. Will you wait for me?"

"You know I will wait for you. I truly love you and want to be your wife," Norma said and began crying.

He took her in his arms and said, "Sweet Norma, I love you so dearly. I never want to make you cry. Take me to visit the farm tomorrow. I want to meet Doll." Frank stroked her hair until she finally stopped crying.

It was well past midnight when Norma showed Frank to the guest bedroom. She barely slept any that night, and Saturday remained a blur the following weeks. Somehow, she always remembered Sunday morning and Frank's goodbye kiss as he drove away.

CHAPTER 9

NOVEMBER 1942

While Norma was dealing with Frank joining the navy and leaving, she was unaware of what was happening in North Africa. On November 8 General George Patton had led American forces on an invasion into North Africa to aid the British who were battling the Italians and the Germans to protect the Suez Canal. Over the next months the fighting was fierce. The German forces were led by Field Marshal Rommel, Germany's most successful and recognized military leader.

Rommel's Africa Korps was expected to defeat the Americans without experiencing very large losses. Among his officers was Dr. Dirk Wagner, who was the young nephew of a friend of his mother. The poor woman had a premonition thar her son would die in the war. Rommel had laughed at her but had welcomed the young Dr. Dirk Wagner to his staff. When the fighting began to go very badly for the Germans, Dr. Wagner asked Rommel's permission to go to the battlefield and treat badly wounded soldiers at field hospitals. The request was granted on March 1,1943 and he shook Rommel's hand for what was to be the last time.

Dr. Wagner was put to work immediately at the first field hospital he found. He was quickly operating eight to ten hours a day. Several weeks passed before he got a day off to rest. After he slept for seven hours, he awoke somewhat rested and walked back to the field hospital. He spoke to a doctor closing a scalp wound. The doctor directed him to the location where the wounded were arriving currently by ambulances, and trucks, as well as, being carried in on stretchers by hospital workers. Just as he reached the point of entry two men were carrying a stretcher through the door. One man dropped one end of the stretcher and collapsed. Wagner grabbed the stretcher before the patient fell to the ground.

"Thank you, Sir. My partner didn't tell me he was shot. He seems to be dead," the other stretcher bearer soldier said.

"The patient you were carrying is dead also," said Wagner.

The soldier turned to leave, and Warner called to him. "Where are you going?"

"I am going back to bring more wounded here, Sir."

"I will come with you. You cannot carry a stretcher by yourself," said Wagner.

"Sir, officers are not stretcher bearers," said the soldier.

"I am one today soldier," answered Wagner.

The two worked several hours, but Wagner became aware that each time they returned to the front line it was moving backward not forward. "Our lines keep moving in the wrong direction. At this rate the field hospital needs to move further back, or it will be overrun," he told the soldier.

The words were barely out of his mouth when a tank came into view and began firing. Both men ducked and hit the ground. When Wagner opened his eyes, he saw his fellow stretcher bearer's body lying by him with his head missing. Without any hesitation Wagner removed his shirt and exchanged it for the dead man's. He searched the man's pants and found his military identification and replaced it with his. He looked at his new identification and knew he was no longer Dirk Wagner, a doctor and personal friend on Rommel's staff, but was now Victor Brandt. He had a better chance of survival as a soldier than as an officer and would be in a better position to help wounded prisoners.

Within less than two minutes he was surrounded by American infantry men and told to raise his hands. He was led away to join a large group of German prisoners and loaded on a truck to be taken to a holding area where several hundred more prisoners were already being searched and interrogated. The next two weeks he saw many more prisoners being shoved into the area, but he was mainly watching the prisoners beginning to group themselves. The officers began gathering away from the enlisted men. The most senior ranking officers took command of them. The leading enlisted men immediately began to collect the men who had been in their units into groups. The few who could not locate any of the men they had been fighting with when they were captured were the group that Wagner joined. He did not want to be recognized as an officer. He also had to be sure that none of Brandt's friends would recognize him as an imposter wearing Brandt's shirt.

When the American captain came to interrogate him, Wagner quickly identified himself as Victor Brandt and admitted to speaking English. He explained that he worked in a field hospital where his primary job was being a stretcher bearer. He did not have a weapon issued to him at any time and had worked in hospitals the entire time he had been in the army. The American captain had listened carefully and had written down all of the details Brandt was telling him before Brandt's name on the chart that he was creating about the prisoners. When the captain moved on to the next prisoner, Brandt began to relax because he knew that his new identity was established.

On May 12, 1943 the Germans officially surrendered all of their forces in North Africa after long months of fighting. Their inevitable loss meant Rommel had left Africa on medical leave in March and had not returned. By this time there were 250,000 German and Italian soldiers, now prisoners, cramped together into designated areas along the African coast. The American and British had to plan how to move them out of Africa. It became clear to Brandt that the Americans would be sending the majority, if not all of these prisoners, to the United States. He was in the second group to be loaded on an American ship headed for the trip to New York. The ship should arrive in about two weeks if a German U-boat did not sink this ship which remained a strong possibility.

Brandt was very surprised when he recognized the ship was approaching New York harbor after a fairly uneventful trip. He had recognized that the ship had been zigzagging across the Atlantic but had not decreased its speed. However, he heard the men around him complaining to each other loudly as the passed the Statue of Liberty, and as well, saw many skyscrapers in Manhattan. They had been told by their superiors that the German Air Force had already bombed New York and other major American cities.

"This city has not been bombed! Why did they lie to us?" asked the prisoner standing closest to Brandt.

"I imagine it was to keep each of us from getting discouraged as we began losing the battle we were fighting," said Brandt. "We must remember we are Germans and must behave in a very civilized manner while we are prisoners here. If we are respectful, I believe the Americans will treat us with respect."

"I joined the German army before the Nazi Party gained control of the country. Are you a Nazi?"

"No. I joined because a friend's mother asked me to join and protect her son. I have not joined the Nazi Party," Brandt answered.

"I didn't think so. I had not seen you joining the group of very dedicated party members. I don't believe they will be interested in being respectful of these Americans. I expect they may get themselves shot."

"Did you not hear the announcement that the Americans will be treating all prisoners who come into U.S. custody in strict compliance with the Geneva Convention? That requires every part of our lives will be monitored, but will be safe and humane," Brandt explained.

"I sure hope you are right. I will wait and see if those are just words, but are actually carried out. I am sure the Nazi will not be as compliant as you and I."

CHAPTER 10

JUNE 1943

After disembarking from the ship and again being interrogated, approximately three hundred men were marched onto a specially prepared train that began the trip to a prison camp. Brandt was in the very last group that was loaded onto the last car of the train. He found a seat with a very young soldier who had a very solemn face. However, Brandt could see his heart rate was racing. "Are you feeling ill?" he asked the young soldier.

"Are they taking us out of the city to shoot us?" he answered.

"We are being taken to the interior of the country to a prison camp where I expect we will be living and working until the end of the war. Don't believe the rumors that we will be slave labor in fields and factories, or that we will be tortured and starved. The Americans have announced that they will be following the dictates of the Geneva Convention that requires humane treatment of all prisoners of war." These were the most reassuring words Brandt could think of so quickly. "I am not sure how long we will be on the train. Why don't you get as comfortable as possible and try to relax and even take a nap."

"I certainly hope you are right. I had hoped the war would end when we defeated the British and entered London. I never imagined being sent to the United States,"

"Well, Hitler was unable to land an army in England and you were not killed in Africa. Now you have a chance to survive the war," Brandt said quietly.

The young soldier looked intently at Brandt and almost smiled but kept his composure and began to breathe easier. Brandt could see that he had helped this kid with his calm words and reassurance. He knew this was part of the reason he needed to be in the prison with these young men and not the officer core of hardened military-minded men.

"I heard the train conductor telling someone that we were going to Aliceville, Alabama as we were getting on the train," the soldier said. "Do you know where that is?"

"You understand English! I believe that will be very useful for you. Sorry, but I don't know much about the geography of this country. I do know it is bigger than England and also bigger than Germany," Brandt answered.

"I guess we will know soon about that Geneva Convention thing you were talking about," the soldier said.

"Yes, we will," Brandt said.

On June 2, 1943 this first train bringing prisoners to Aliceville arrived at about five o'clock and stopped at the street that went directly down the road to the prison camp that was about two miles away. Trains passed through Aliceville several times each day but never stopped. However, today was different! The people had been told by the military to stay at home, but both sides of the street were lined with people. Some were sitting on the hoods of cars, some were standing on the porches of houses, and a few older boys had climbed into trees. Many even had cameras and were ready to take pictures of the German prisoners who they had only seen in newsreels at the movies.

Norma had driven her parents to a friend's house on this main street and they were seated on the front porch waiting.

"You know these are Rommel's Afrika Korps veterans. They are seasoned fighters and probably the very best in the German Army," said George.

"I knew you would want to be here. It was a good idea to close the store early," said Norma.

"All the stores were closing early. We have been waiting a long time for prisoners to arrive," George answered his daughter.

Looking past the army trucks and the Red Cross ambulance, Norma saw armed military guards posted on the platform awaiting the prisoners. The crowd heard a loud train whistle as the train slowed and stopped. She didn't realize she caught her breath when she saw the prisoners for the first time as they stepped from the train. They formed into rows and began marching down the street. The armed Americans lined up on both sides of the prisoners and marched in step with them.

As they began marching the prisoners began singing a militant marching song in German. The crowd remained quiet as they looked at the tired, ragged, mostly young men goose-stepping their way to prison.

"These young men even look younger than Ben," said Florence.

"They may look young, but they are experienced and well- trained soldiers. I am glad they are here and not still on the battlefield facing men like our son Ben, who has no actual experience in a battle," said George.

As the prisoners approached the front gate of the prison, Norma helped her parents back into her car and drove them home. "I was told that about three hundred would arrive today and that within the next few days more than three thousand prisoners will have arrived. I will be reporting to work tomorrow at 8am and will not be home until after 4pm. I am going to try to get myself put on the night shift or swing shift if possible so I will be at home during the day."

"You just work when they need you. These prisoners need you more than your dad and I need you right now. I saw bloody bandages, and some were limping. "We can always call you if something happens at the store," said Florence.

Norma left for work the next morning and began an adventure that would influence the rest of her life in ways she could not even imagine.

CHAPTER 11

When the prison came into view, the prisoners each took a quick look. The watch towers were very prominent, and the wire fences were very tall. They realized this place was certainly a well-planned facility, not like the makeshift stockades they had left in Africa.

When the march stopped at the main gate, an American walked from the front to the back asking if any of the men spoke English. Brandt spoke quietly to the soldier he had sat by on the train. "This is your chance to become significant. Speak up now."

The young man answered. "Sir, I speak English."

"Good. Follow me to the front. You can tell the rest of the prisoners what they need to know as they enter the camp. What is your name?"

"I am Felix Fischer," he answered. "Are we going to be shot now?"

The American looked surprised and then smiled. "Felix, do you see this camp. Does it make sense that we would build this place if we planned to just shoot all of you?"

"I see it, but we were told we would be shot if captured," he answered.

The American just shook his head in disbelief. "Felix, please tell them to proceed into the camp in single file formation and state their name clearly to the man holding the roster of their names. He will then send each one into the inner fence and process them into one of the six separately fenced compounds that are here. Tell them this will be done as quickly as possible," the American stated.

Felix loudly explained the process to be followed and the Germans immediately began moving forward in one line. It took hours to process the prisoners who entered into the camp. It was after two in the morning when temporary cooks finally stopped serving coffee to both prisoners and base camp workers. Each prisoner had been assigned to a specific fenced compound and was moved into one of these where there were ten barracks on each side of a rutted roadway with two lavatory buildings behind each row of barracks.

Brandt had maneuvered himself so that he was the last prisoner to enter. He and Felix also entered to be processed. They were both assigned to the same compound. They entered into their barracks to see fifty sturdy cots with twenty-five on each side. The cots were made up of sheets, army blankets tucked tightly under the thin mattresses, and pillows inside ironed pillowcases. Each cot had a toothbrush, a tube of toothpaste, shaving cream, a razor and a bar of soap placed on top of the pillow. They took the first two cots available and sat down. Both were completely exhausted. Most of the prisoners in this barracks were leaving going in the compound mess hall for food, but Brandt and Felix headed to the lavatory behind their barracks for a hot shower and shave before dressing in their prison uniforms and coming back into their barracks. They slept better than they had since before they had been taken as prisoners in North Africa.

The following morning, they visited all of the buildings that made up their compound. They found ten barracks, a small infirmary, a post exchange, a recreational building, a maintenance shop, and the mess hall. In the mess hall they received a breakfast of coffee and white bread spread with something that Felix had never seen before. "Brandt, do you know what this is?"

"It is an American concoction that I think you will like," Brandt answered.

"Have you ever, had it?" Felix asked.

"One of the doctors who worked at the hospital where I worked in Berlin brought some back when he visited a hospital here in the States. Everyone who tried it really liked it. Try it. It is called peanut butter," said Brandt as he took a big bite.

Felix watched him chew and took a bite as well. He carefully thought about what he was chewing before saying, "I like the peanut butter better than I like the bread, but the bread is better with it than it would be alone."

"It is better than being hungry for sure. We have both been hungry many times in the past two years or more. You won't ever hear me complain about the food we are given," Brandt reminded Felix.

Another prisoner opened the door and spoke loudly enough that everyone in the building could hear him. "More prisoners are just arriving. Our compound is not full. We may be getting more men."

"What is our compound number?" asked Felix.

"We are in Compound A," answered Brandt. "I asked the army doctor who was checking on the health of each prisoner last night, and he said each compound could house one thousand prisoners. There were only around three hundred on the train we were on. Certainly, there will be more assigned into this compound."

After they finished breakfast both Brandt and Felix joined a large group of prisoners standing close to the locked gate of their compound. They were watching several new prisoners being escorted to the gate by an armed guard. The guard unlocked the gate and sent the new members into the compound before relocking it. Felix pushed forward and reminded these new members that the place where the other prisoners were watching them was as close to the locked gate as was allowed. He pointed to the tower where armed guards were stationed and had a clear view of the gate of this compound. The new members quickly moved to join the men in the appropriate position and were greeted by the German Noncommissioned officer who had become the compound leader who led them away to determine which barracks to assign these newest members.

By this time all the prisoners in compound A had showered and changed out of their ragged, torn, bloody and very dirty clothes and were dressed in the denim pants and shirts with the white five-inch- tall painted letters "PW" on the back of each shirt. The camp workers had selected the size each prisoner needed during the processing. A few had rolled their pants up some, but Brant saw no one in clothes that were too small.

Trains continued arriving all day. The prisoners finally quit standing around looking at the new soldiers being led by armed guards to Compounds A, B, and C. Brandt was talking to the man who had taken the cot next to him about when he had arrived in North Africa when the barrack door opened, and an armed guard called Brandt's name. Brandt rose from his cot and stepped out to the foot of it, faced the guard, and gave the Nazi salute. He did this to demonstrate to the other prisoners how to respond when being singled out. He didn't believe he had broken any rules and hoped no one had identified him as an officer and personal friend of Rommel, who had assumed a dead soldier's rank and name.

The guard motioned Brandt to follow him from the barracks. When they were clear of the area Brandt had a great desire to ask where they were going, but he assumed that the guard would not respond. He grew more concerned when he saw that he was being taken in the direction of the main headquarters building away from the compound. However, when this building was passed, he wondered if there was a stand- alone interrogation building. When suddenly the guard stopped and motioned Brandt to enter.

Brandt approached the door and relaxed when he saw the word "Hospital" stenciled on the door. He pushed the door open and was met by the doctor he had spoken to while being processed into the camp. He smiled and said, "You remembered my name."

"It was the first thought I had when the number of patients we have this morning was ten times what we had when I left last night. You told me you had worked in hospitals before and since you had been the army, and I knew you spoke excellent English. You can certainly help us today!"

"Thank you, Sir. I will do my best to help. What do you need me to do first?" asked Brandt.

"First, let me introduce you to the nurse you will be assisting today," the doctor said as he turned and called the nurse. "Nurse Fleming, come and meet the orderly you will be working with today."

Brandt looked in the direction of the doctor who called the nurse. He saw a tall blonde with azure blue eyes and a gorgeous smiling mouth walking toward him. He had known many beautiful women in his thirty-three years but had never worked with a nurse who was this stunning. He knew he was staring but could not look away.

"Nurse Fleming this is Victor Brandt. He was working in a Berlin hospital before joining the German army and was working in a field hospital when he was taken prisoner in North Africa. He is being assigned to work with you today," said the doctor.

"Good morning," she said without offering a smile or handshake.

"Good morning," Brandt answered and thought this relationship has a long way to go to ever become cordial.

"You must speak English, because I don't know any German," the nurse said.

"Yes, I speak English. I visited relatives in England many times before the war."

"Let's begin with this patient that I need you to lift and turn so I can lance a boil on his back," she spoke as she hurried toward the patient.

Brandt enjoyed looking at the back of Nurse Fleming as he followed her. He realized it had been too long since he had seen a woman, but decided this one was going to be all business. He reminded himself this hospital was in a prison camp, and he was a prisoner. He tried to remember that fact as he and Nurse Fleming worked together all day.

CHAPTER 12

JUNE 1943

John and James Webb were enjoying a slow start on the first Saturday in June. They had returned late last night from New Orleans, and now sat in their studio having their morning coffee and talking about their successes in the time they had lived in Panama City, Florida.

"It doesn't seem like we have been here this long. How many pictures would you estimate we have taken?" James asked.

"If you are asking about here in the studio, I would guess at least between five hundred and six hundred. Those specials we advertised in June making graduation pictures have been very successful, and the wedding pictures for the newspaper have been the icing on the cake," John responded.

"Yes, I agree but I was really asking about the pictures we have been taking to New Orleans."

"It hasn't been that many for sure, but I think we are fulfilling our mission with more than the expected numbers. Let's see, we took the first pictures at Tyndall Airfield in early 1942 and returned late in the year when the military started gunnery training there. I think we used a whole roll of film on each trip.

"I remember we were anxious when that military police car stopped us and asked what we were doing so close to the base with cameras and you answered that we were trying to get a picture of Clark Gable who was stationed there," laughed James.

"I remember telling him that having a picture of Clark Gable in our Photography Shop would bring in more business, and he bought it!"

"Thank goodness a famous movie star was going through gunnery school here," James added.

"Remember those pictures were the first we took to New Orleans where we met our contact. He is quite an unusual person. A Mexican who is being paid to carry information and pictures from the U. S. to a German spy in Argentina was not what either of us expected. That is a long trip. He has to be making very good money to make that round trip as often as he seems to," said John.

"Then we planned a trip to Pensacola where the navy trains pilots and stopped off at Eglin Field on the way. Too bad we missed the opportunity to get pictures of Doolittle Raiders training for that raid on Tokyo, but we did get good pictures of the field and the surrounding area," James said. "The pictures of planes in the air over Pensacola were great and the road leading to the main gate shows the surrounding area."

"I think the best pictures we took on the trip were of the Mobile harbor where the ships were docked. I had no idea that that harbor had so much potential. I know that area is not as well- known as New Orleans, but it may be a critical area also," John stated.

"I believe we are being very successful so far. I am not sure whether we should be focusing now on possible areas for an invasion force to use. We will have to listen very carefully tonight when we are out in bars and ask some leading questions when the local patrons have had several drinks. Make sure we both have the money to keep buying drinks, especially if we begin to get good information," said James.

"Don't I always? The answer to your question about the number of pictures and the narratives we have included with each package we have sent seems to be about thirty or forty pictures. I am not sure how long it takes to get from New Orleans to Berlin. I do believe the intelligence we are sending means our families are receiving our pay checks and are doing well," said John.

That night John and James heard about a prison camp in Aliceville, Alabama with thousands of German prisoners who had been captured in

North Africa. They decided that their next trip might have to be a trip to Aliceville, Alabama!

CHAPTER 13

JULY 1943

Norma's first days in the hospital were very busy. It seemed that more patients arrived every day. One day a large number of stretchers were brought in, and Norma became the triage nurse deciding where these patients were to be placed for their treatment. It quickly became clear to her that more personnel were needed. Luckily, a group of German doctors who were prisoners arrived at this camp at the perfect time. Col. Prince decided to house them in the area that had been preserved for a psychiatric ward that had no patients. It was inappropriate to have officers in the barracks which were designed for enlisted men. Also, they were issued white coats to wear and not required to wear denim pants and shirts with the "PW" on the back. They began working immediately on their arrival caring for the patients that the senior American doctor assigned each one. Norma noticed that Brandt appeared to be very busy and made no effort to interact with the German doctors. She wondered why, but she was too busy to question him.

At the end of the shift, she did hear Brandt asking the senior doctor to transfer him to another shift if possible. He said he would not be needed to translate for the patients with so many German doctors assigned to this shift. That seemed a reasonable request, and he was told a new schedule was being prepared to include the additional doctors. He would be placed where he would be most needed. She knew she wanted to work the same shift Brandt worked, but she didn't want to ask immediately after his request.

She decided to just wait until the new schedule was made available. The following morning, she saw Brandt was not working. She wondered how he had managed to get himself moved so quickly, or if he had gotten sick himself. Either way she missed him and hoped to find out the reason he was not there. She knew she wanted to continue working at this hospital, but she did not enjoy assisting a German even if he was a doctor. After a few days she asked to be transferred to the swing shift. She had seen Brandt constantly working the swing shift and used her parents and their needs as her reason to change shifts.

Soon she was enjoying her work at the camp hospital again. Now she walked her dad to the hardware store to start the day. She could work in the office while he was getting the coffee pot working and the store ready to open. She helped serve customers or worked on the office books until she walked her dad back home for lunch. She stayed home after her dad headed back to the store to help her mother with any housework that needed to be done. Then she would usually wash clothes and iron her nurse uniform, before going up to her room, to read, nap, or write a letter to Frank or her brother. She came downstairs dressed for work and helped her mother prepare the night meal before she left to go to the camp hospital.

Of course, this schedule meant she had no time to go to the farm to ride Doll during the week. Therefore, every Saturday morning, she walked her dad to the store and headed to the farm where she spent time riding Doll while checking on the farm fences, the crops, the outbuildings and even the farm equipment. On Sunday the family went to church and Sunday school, and they spent the rest of the day quietly at home. This peaceful day allowed Norma to be rejuvenated for the upcoming week.

On Monday afternoon she was rested and happy to be coming back to work. She worked well with Brandt because none of the other orderlies were as trained and as knowledgeable as he. She was glad when she arrived and saw that he was standing by a bed speaking German to a prisoner. The prisoner's head was bandaged. There was an eye patch covering his right eye and his right arm was in a cast. Brandt was holding that right hand. When Brandt saw her, he left the patient and came over to her.

"Good afternoon, Nurse Fleming, we have a very different case today. I was called in early this morning when this prisoner was found unconscious in his barracks. He was attacked last night by one or more prisoners. The Commander is determined to find out which prisoner or prisoners almost killed him, but he has refused to identify anyone. I have been trying to explain how important this information is."

"Is he confused or just reluctant to talk?" she asked.

"He is very coherent; however, I haven't determined if he is unaware of who the man or men were, or he is simply afraid."

"Just keep checking his vital signs at regular intervals and keep me informed," she said.

Norma moved toward a patient who had been sedated because he had been told that his right foot would have to be amputated and he had become almost hysterical. He had raved that the American doctor just wanted to mutilate him. Norma knew that his injured foot had not been treated correctly in Africa where the injury had occurred and the infection that followed had not responded to the treatment he had received when he arrived at the camp. It would spread further if the foot was not amputated right away. One of the German doctors was the one who ordered that he be sedated without attempting to make him understand. His surgery was scheduled for 8 am in the morning.

She moved from him to another patient recovering from surgery, who smiled at her and asked for something to drink, by pointing his thumb at his open mouth. She nodded and brought him a glass of water with a straw. She continued her rounds among the many very sick and those who were recovering nicely and would soon be leaving the hospital and returning to their compound. It appeared to be a normal day at work.

That all changed when she saw Brandt coming back into the hospital and immediately going to the leading doctor on duty. They had a short conversation before Brandt moved back to the patient with the head bandaged and the broken arm and began talking to him in German. She had not been aware that Brandt had left the hospital and wondered where he had gone. The look on his face was very concerning to her and she carefully walked over to him.

"How are his vital signs; are they still normal?" she asked.

"Yes, but he needed reassurance that he didn't have to worry about returning to his compound after his time in the hospital is over. I have been in the Headquarters talking to Col. Prince about what he finally told me about the attack," Brandt answered.

"Oh, I see," Norma said. "It obviously helps that these young men will trust you."

"I think it is clear that I am older than the majority of the prisoners that are here, and I have to make them aware that cooperating with you, Americans, is to their advantage. It would be hard for you to imagine how strange it is to be this far away from Europe and all the world they have ever known."

"It was Germany that started this war. Certainly, the United States didn't want to get involved in another war," she stated.

"Is your husband somewhere fighting?" he asked.

"I am not married, but my fiancé is on a ship in the Pacific," she answered.

"I hope he is safe, Nurse Fleming," Brandt softly answered and turned back to continue his duties.

Norma watched him walk away from her. She certainly had not intended to share any of her personal life with any of the German prisoners, but she was beginning to think of Brandt differently. He was always very gentle and caring with the patients, extremely professional, and very careful to listen to the nurses and doctors before carrying out their orders faultlessly. She finally admitted to herself that she actually liked at least this one German!

CHAPTER 14

On her way home after work that night, Norma remembered that Brandt had not told her anything about what the injured patient had told him about his attackers. They had both actually talked about personal feelings. That was not what she had ever expected to share with a German prisoner. She knew their conversation had seemed to be very natural and certainly not provocative, but she admitted they had shared information about their lives as equals. However, working together for hours each day would mean their relationship would inevitably change. She knew it was up to her to keep the relationship professional.

When she arrived at the front door, she quietly entered to keep from waking her parents. She removed her shoes before climbing the stairs to her room. Once inside she turned on the lights and got out pen and paper to write Frank. She wrote her usual "love you, miss you" and had little else to say. Her daily routine didn't change, and the censors read anything she wrote anyway, so this was a very short letter. She did write that she would call his sister in Nashville and inquire about his parents and the rest of his family. She knew she had been remiss in not keeping in touch with them. When she sealed the letter, she collapsed on her bed and slept in her clothes that night!

When Norma arrived at the camp the next afternoon, her eyes searched for Brandt, but she didn't see him. She did see the doctor on duty and approached him. "Dr. Johnson is Brandt back at the Headquarters again?" she asked.

"No. He is on the schedule to work the overnight shift. He took the shift Carter usually works because his wife went into labor in Tuscaloosa and Carter wanted to go and be there when the baby is born. Brandt was the first-person Carter thought of and Brandt, of course, was very happy to take the shift. He told Carter he could work that shift as long as Carter wanted to take time off to be with his wife and new baby. Brandt is liked by all the prisoners who have become patients here, as well as the guys on the staff here," the doctor answered.

"Does Carter and his wife live in Tuscaloosa? He has a long drive every day to come to work here."

"Yes, he does. There are just not enough places to live here in Aliceville, and both he and his wife wanted to have a doctor deliver their child in a hospital. Poor old Carter knows just enough medicine to be anxious about his wife," said Dr. Johnson.

"That was very kind of Brandt. He and many of the prisoners seem like nice people," Norma said.

"There are a few Nazi Party members mixed in with the others and they are much more rigid in the interactions with all staff officers here. They still believe this war will be won by the Axis Powers and feel very superior. They are much harder to like than the other prisoners," Dr. Johnson added.

"Well, it is time for me to go to work. Without Brandt here, I will have to keep a close eye on the other workers this evening. Sometimes they aren't as diligent as I am," Norma said as she placed her purse in her locker and hurried out to the hospital floor.

For the next several hours she concentrated seriously on her job. Then everything started to slow down as it approached ten pm. The lights dimmed and some of the patients began to prepare to go to sleep. Norma got a cup of coffee and sat down at the front desk. Actually, this shift had not been as hectic as many other evenings she spent at the hospital, but she had missed Brandt anyway. She hoped the Carter baby had arrived safely by this time and was sleeping in the hospital nursery. She looked up when she sensed someone was standing by her. It was Brandt with a broad smile on his face. She smiled back.

"I wasn't expecting you for another hour," she said.

"If I had waited until then, you would be leaving, and I would have to begin working. We would have no time to talk," he answered.

"You were very kind to swap shifts with Carter," she said.

"It was certainly the right thing to do. If I were married, I hope someone would swap with me if my wife was having our child."

"You are not married?" Norma asked.

"No. I knew several lovely ladies in Berlin. My mother even picked out one she wanted me to marry, before she died, but I was busy working. Finding the right lady to marry would have taken more time than I could afford. I know that must sound self-centered, but it is true. I believe I will find the right one for me some day. I may look older because of this war, but I am only thirty-three. I still have time to fall in love and expect to have a wonderful married life with children and grandchildren," Brandt explained.

"As soon as this war is over, I will be getting married. My fiancé is a dentist and part owner of a dental business. We would probably have set a date for our wedding by this time, but this war interrupted our lives. I am only here in Aliceville because my younger brother joined the army, and I had to come and help my parents until he returns."

"Nurse Fleming, you have a very lucky fiancé. His wife-to-be is not only very beautiful, but she is a very smart nurse who will always make him very proud," said Brandt.

Before Norma could reply, the nurse coming to work this shift came rushing in. "Norma, tell me that I am not late. My husband and I went to the movies and the newsreel were much longer than usual, but I hurried right over."

"Heather, you are not late! This is Brandt. He will be working with you tonight. Carter is in Tuscaloosa. His wife is having their first child right now and Brandt volunteered to come in and replace him."

"Hello, Brandt. I am Nurse Heather Baldwin. I know we will work together fine," Heather said and hurried to put up her purse.

When Norma and Brandt were alone together, he spoke so softly than only Norma heard him say, "Goodnight, Nurse Norma."

It was the first time he had ever called her by her first name. She didn't answer because she didn't remember Brandt's first name. She knew, without a doubt, she would know it by this time tomorrow.

CHAPTER 15

Brandt had been afraid he might be recognized by the German doctors who had suddenly appeared in the hospital. He had to stay as far away from them as possible and worked to keep his back turned. Of course, they would not expect to see him as an enlisted prisoner here at Aliceville, but if they did recognize him, he was unsure of what the repercussions might be. He did not want the Americans to think he had been planted in with the enlisted to observe their treatment, or that he was a close friend of Rommel. Either of these possible outcomes could have cost him dearly no matter how he reacted to being found out. Thankfully, he did not know any of the doctors and they did not appear to know him. He had managed to be changed to the swing shift and now was working the overnight shift because another orderly asked him to switch with him. He hoped the German doctors would avoid this overnight shift.

He had regretted not working with Nurse Fleming until she changed to the swing shift as well. Both of them had become a team and seemed to almost always to be on the same wavelength when approaching any patient. Tonight, since he was working the overnight shift, he had come in early to engage in a conversation with her that had allowed him to learn she was not married, and her first name was Norma. This was certainly more personal information than he had gained while both were on the day shift or the swing shift. It actually made him more determined to learn even more about Norma Fleming.

The next morning when he left the hospital, he went to his compound to get breakfast. One cook was there and ready to serve him. Over the next week they met every morning and both men got to know each other better. Brandt learned that this new friend, Stefan Hesse, had been a chef at a nice restaurant in Cologne. He admitted he was forced to join the army when the Gestapo came to the restaurant. He went on to say he had never been political and was enjoying being able to cook again even if the ingredients weren't what he most enjoyed using. Brant used this opportunity to ask if Stefan knew which soldiers in their compound were Nazi.

Stefan answered, "The ones who complain most about the food and the lack of beer!"

"I will listen carefully to hear their complaints. The Nazi have been attacking the prisoners who have been cooperative with the Americans. It would mean fewer patients in the hospital if the more virulent Nazi were transferred away from here. I currently have a patient who was bashed on the head with a rock, a kitchen knife was jammed into his eye, and his arm broken. He has been treated more kindly by his captors than by his countrymen," Brandt stated.

"Have you met any of the German doctors who are here now? I have heard that they don't have to wear our prison uniform and are even allowed to leave the camp and walk into the town. Do you think that is true?" asked Stefan.

"They are not in prison uniforms in the hospital and probably are allowed to leave the camp. I expect they realize that they have very little chance of escape and do not want to be caught trying. Their treatment is quite good now and attempted escape would probably mean much less freedom," Brandt answered.

As he made his way back to his barracks Brandt wondered how long the war would last. He did not regret the decision he had made on the battlefield to change his uniform and become an enlisted man instead of an officer. He knew he had helped many of the young men, who were just nineteen or twenty, deal with spending part of their youth as prisoners. He did miss being a real doctor who actually made decisions and brought about healing. The German doctors who were working in the camp hospital made him miss his chosen career more than ever. If he had any inkling that the Americans would have allowed German doctors to practice medicine while remaining prisoners, he wondered if he might have not reacted as quickly as he had done when he saw the soldier whose head had been blown off lying by him. All of that was water under the bridge now, and he knew he would live out the path he had taken that day in Africa.

He listened to his barracks' mates that afternoon and early evening to hear if anyone was complaining about no beer or the poor quality and food they were being served. He knew everyone had not wanted to eat corn, which was pig food in Germany. The cooks had managed to explain to the camp workers not to bring any more so that every mess hall in the camp got no more corn and more potatoes going forward. However, he didn't hear any complaints. This evening the prisoners were all talking about track and field areas that were being created so that they could compete in athletic events. Brandt smiled to hear these young men sounding so positive.

That positive attitude was continuing to grow when Col. Prince had been diligently working to ensure that beer would be available in the camp canteens. This was amazing since beer was not available in dry Pickens County.

The prisoners had become more creative as time passed. They had been busy decorating the areas in front of their barracks with whatever materials they had or found. Some were creating musical instruments, and one began teaching English classes. This did not keep all of them busy, and they hoped for work. Col. Prince decided until the ordered caps or hats arrived, he would not allow them to work outside on farms because of the heat in the Alabama summer. Brandt knew that idle hands would not be good for the harmony that was developing between the prisoners and their captors, and he watched both groups daily. Brandt worked for Carter for only one week, but that week he always went to the hospital an hour early to get to see Nurse Norma. Even when she was too busy to spend any time talking to him, he got to watch her treat the German prisoners who were patients as kindly and gently as she treated the American soldiers who were patients. He realized that he was admiring her skills as a nurse, and her character, as well as her extraordinary beauty.

He had to admit to himself that he was falling in love with this American nurse. He began to hope that the war would end very soon. He wanted to tell her the truth about who he was and perhaps she could be persuaded that their friendship could grow. He remembered she had told him that she was engaged to a dentist who was onboard a ship in the Pacific fighting the Japanese. He would not disclose his love for her as long as her fiancé was in the picture, but he told himself that he would probably like the man if she was in love with him. This war had certainly complicated everyone's life. He wondered what the world would be like when the war ended but knew there were too many variables to arrive at any conclusions at this time about his own life, and even less about the whole world!

CHAPTER 16

Finally, the day arrived when the prisoners were allowed to begin working outside of the prison. The Geneva Convention requirements had strict rules concerning how prisoners were to be treated both inside the prison camp and outside. The local sawmill wanted workers to fell trees which required a review by the powers that be because the Geneva convention was basically opposed to prisoners working in the forest industry both in felling trees and in sawmills. However, after the explanation that these southern trees were small, never over eight inches in circumference, permission was granted. A large group of prisoners received training on the work they would be doing in the forest and at the sawmill. They learned quickly and soon the mill was working at full capacity and the number of guards needed to watch them working was reduced. This work continued almost to the day the prisoners were sent back to England and then on to Germany.

The prisoners also began doing work on the surrounding farms and even went as far as the areas in southeastern Alabama where peanuts were the main crop. There was no doubt that the majority of the peanut crop would be lost without the help the prisoners provided. Local farmers were not disregarded and many requested prisoner workers when harvesting and planting. Norma's father decided he would request a worker for his farm and was surprised by how quickly he was given the name of the prisoner who had been assigned to him. He asked Norma to interview the German before accepting him as a farm hand.

Norma went to work early the following morning and asked Brandt to sit with her in the interview before she made a decision about telling her father that the prisoner was a good choice for the family farm. When the prisoner arrived at the hospital, Brandt spoke to him in German and took him into an examining room. Norma quickly joined in and introduced herself.

"Good morning, I am Nurse Fleming. I don't remember seeing you in the hospital before."

"I am here no time," the prisoner answered.

"He told me his English is limited, and asked to work where he could use the language and improve. His name is Karl Baur," said Brandt.

"That is good news. I am certainly happy I asked you to be here to insure we both understand each other," Norma responded to Brandt. Then looking at the prisoner she said, "Karl, tell me all about yourself before the war."

"I live on a small farm in Bavaria. All time I live on a farm. I have two sisters. One married and moved to other farm. One sister too little. Her, uh, she go school," he answered.

"Is your father running the farm while you are in the army?" Norma asked.

"No, Father die in war in France," the prisoner answered.

Brandt immediately began speaking to the prisoner in German and Norma listened to the two men carry on a short conversation. Brandt finally turned to her and said," His father died in 1917. His mother remarried in 1920, and his sisters were both born in the early years of the 1920's. One is married and one is retarded and must attend a special program. This man is 30 years old and not married. He only joined the army because the farm was barely providing for the family. That may have been the reason the other sister got married. "

"Oh, I am so sorry. I know my parents will want to help him," Norma said. "How old is his retarded sister?"

"He is very careful what he will share about her. You may not know that the Nazi Party had a policy to remove any German who was born physically or mentally damaged starting in the 1930's and only stopped in 1941," Brandt said.

"What do you mean by removed?" Norma asked.

"Norma, forgive me for having to tell you, but they were usually killed by means that were as painless as possible. Hitler was planning on creating a superior race."

"Oh Lord, I had no idea. I knew that Jews were arrested, and many fled the country. I had no idea they murdered their own citizens," Norma almost whispered.

"Norma, I am so sorry that you had to learn this from me. I assure you many, many Germans were unaware, and others were too afraid for their own lives to speak up. You must know I was never a Nazi," Brandt said.

Karl had been listening to Brandt and Norma quietly talking. He spoke up in German to Brandt.

Brandt answered him then spoke to Norma, "Karl is concerned that what I have told you will prevent you from accepting him as a worker on your farm."

Norma turned to Karl and said, "I can tell you that you will be working at my father's farm beginning tomorrow. Do not worry. I have wonderful parents and they will want you to learn what kind of people we Americans are. We cherish our freedom and respect human life.

The following morning Norma's father arrived at the camp before 9am and Karl Braun was escorted out of the prison by Brandt. George Fleming came forward and spoke to Karl. "Good morning. You will be working at my farm beginning today. Get in my truck and I will drive you there."

Karl nodded and started to climb into the back of the truck when George opened the door to the passenger side and motioned for Braun to get in. George looked at Brandt as he walked around the front of the truck to enter the driver's side and said, "He will be easier for me to keep an eye on him in the cab with me than in the back."

"I would be very surprised if he were to try to escape. I believe he will be quite happy working on a farm. He lived on a farm before the war and will enjoy being back around animals and fields. Nurse Fleming must have told you all about our conversation with him yesterday," Brandt said.

"Yes, she did. I will be staying at the farm until I return him here when my daughter comes to work. He will have to show the family that live on the farm that he will be a good worker who can be depended on before I decide to have him continue working for me. I hope it works out because the family at the farm are getting older just like me and my wife and can surely use the help."

George Fleming started the truck, waved goodbye to Brandt, and headed toward the farm. "The farm is about a ten minute drive from the prison. You will be working for Mr. Milton Bowen and his wife Wilma. They have lived on and worked this farm for many years for me. I will be staying all day to see how this is going to work out. If Milton and Wilma are satisfied, we will continue your working here for some time."

"Thank you, Sir. I like work farm," Karl said.

George chuckled and said, "So do I."

CHAPTER 17

George Fleming had insisted on driving the German prisoner for his first day at work on the farm. Norma had discouraged both of her parents from driving since she had returned to Aliceville, but she recognized that her father was not going to accept her driving the prisoner. She had watched her dad drive away from the house while saying a prayer that the Lord would protect him as well as the prisoner.

Her mother stood at the front door watching Norma standing in the front yard watching her father drive down the road and finally opened the door and said, "Norma, your father can drive to the farm blindfolded. You need to go open the store like you told him you would."

"Okay, Mom. I just don't want to be responsible for dad having an accident. I am not sure my brother would ever forgive me. For that matter, I couldn't forgive myself."

"He told you he could drive, didn't he?"

"Yes, of course, and I know he was kidding when he said he just couldn't see any more," added Norma.

"He sees just fine. Now, hurry on to the store. He will be disappointed if you are late getting it opened," Florence said as she turned away from the door and went to get another cup of coffee.

Norma did get the door unlocked and the open sign hung up in the hardware store on time. The regular morning customers began arriving and gathered around the pot-bellied stove, but without her father being present she saw that they left much sooner than usual.

She laughed to herself and sat down on the high stool behind the cash register with a romance novel to read when a man she didn't recognize walked in. "Good morning, Can I help you?" she asked.

"A screw worked its way out of my tripod. I just need a replacement. I brought the leg with me. Mind if I try finding a screw that will fit it?"

"Oh, sure. The bins holding screws are on that second aisle. Help yourself."

Shortly he came to the cash register with two boxes of screws. "This one seems to fit, but I will buy the next size also just to be sure," he said as he placed the boxes on the counter smiled and said, "How much will this be?"

"You owe me 25 cents. Say, do you live around here? I used to know just about everyone who lived in or around Aliceville, but since they built the prison camp, we have new people moving in and out all the time," Norma said.

"No, my brother and I live in Florida. We heard talk about the prison camp here and drove up. We plan to take some pictures of the prison camp. We are photographers and hopefully will be able to sell them as souvenirs to the locals. We have to be creative to make a living these days."

"Having a prison camp full of Germans here is certainly not anything I ever expected to see. However, this war has impacted every American whether in the military or just a civilian," Norma said.

"My brother and I took pictures of Tyndall Field in Panama City and actually have a picture of it hanging in our studio. We actually took a picture of Clark Gable while he was there and have it in our studio as well. Have you had any famous people visit here in Aliceville?" he asked.

"I am not familiar with any celebrities visiting here. Some may have visited the surrounding farms or even the sawmill, but I am unaware of that."

"The prisoners leave the prison to work in the community?" he asked.

"Yes. With so many men gone to the war, the prisoners are working in the sawmill and on the farms planting and harvesting. Some German doctors are working in the camp hospital. I actually work in the base hospital five days every week. I am only here today because it is a Saturday."

The front door opened, and a second man entered. He came over to the cash register where Norma and the first man were standing. The first man looked up at him and said, "I am sorry it is taking so long, but I have been learning about the prison camp that is here."

The second man smiled then looked at Norma and said, "Hello, I am James, John's brother."

"I am sorry," the first man said, "I did not introduce myself. I am John Webb and my brother has just introduced himself."

"I am Norma Fleming. I hope you both enjoy your visit to Aliceville and Fleming Hardware is ready to provide any tools, parts, equipment, or other assistance you need while you are here. "

"Thank you. We are going over to that drugstore across the street and get some refreshment before we head out to see the prison camp," James said.

Norma watched the men leave and head across the street. She certainly hadn't expected to meet two photographers today. She wondered if anyone in town would buy a picture of the prison camp. Would anyone want to remember the war years and the prison camp?

John and James each had a chocolate malt and then got in their car and headed to the prison camp. They saw the watch towers and the double fences separated by a wide area. No prisoners were close enough to be seen even through their best camera lens, so they decided to get a room and think about how to gain more information and possibly meet some of the prisoners.

They began looking for a place to stay and ended up in Tuscaloosa, Alabama before a hotel room was available. That night they ate in a small restaurant and spoke with their waitress about what she knew about the prison camp in Aliceville. Much to their disappointment she only knew that there was a prison camp in Aliceville. She asked them how far away Aliceville was, so they just went back to the hotel and went to bed.

Tomorrow they would drive back to Aliceville and somehow find a way to talk to some of the prisoners and take some pictures. They would stay here as long as necessary because this trip had to be successful. Surely, German prisoners needed to know there would be help if they could escape this internment camp and needed help in finding how to make their way back home.

CHAPTER 18

Karl Braun made himself very helpful at the Fleming farm. Within two days Milton let George know that he was very satisfied with Braun's work and suggested that he drive to the prison to pick up Karl so that George could just go to the hardware store every morning instead of Norma having to wake up so early or just stay up when she got home from working at the prison hospital. Norma was thrilled when her father agreed to the plan and the prison was notified and accepted Milton Bowen as the man who would pick up Karl Braun and return him at the end of the day.

After almost a week of coming and going from the farm, Milton noticed the same old car parked across the street from the prison with two men sitting inside. He got out of his truck and walked toward the car. As he approached it, the driver got out and spoke. "Hello, I have noticed you bring a prisoner back to the camp every afternoon. Does he work at your business?"

"Are you with the government?" asked Milton.

"Oh, my goodness no. I am a photographer and have been trying to take some pictures of the prisoners and the local citizens. I have been in this area for over a week and have gotten a few pictures with my special lens, but I really want some closer pictures if possible. I think people will like to buy pictures of themselves working here after the war."

"Has the Commander here, given you permission to take pictures?" Milton asked.

"I have not asked for permission. Do you think I should ask permission?"

"I have no doubt. I expect you should move along now. I sure don't want you taking my picture, or a picture of my truck parked here," Milton said.

Just at that moment Norma drove up because it was approaching the time for her to come to work. She saw Milton and waved to him. He waved back and James Webb saw her as well. He called to her,

"Hello, Miss Fleming nice to see you again."

"Hello, I am surprised to see you. I thought you had gone back to Florida by now. Have you taken lots of pictures of the prison camp?"

"Not as many as I had hoped to take. The workers get out of their cars and hurry in. The back of their heads don't make very good pictures and the prisoners don't come close to the gates or fences. We have just about given up. I just asked this gentleman if I could take his picture and he clearly told me no. Usually the workers or military men leave in groups and are talking to each other as they hurry away. Would you let me take your picture over by the gate before you enter?"

"I don't think I should be too close to the gate, but I will stand at the edge of the parking lot and you can take my picture," Norma answered.

"Thank you, Miss Fleming." James reached through the car window and brought out one of his cameras. He followed Norma to the edge of the parking lot. He pointed the camera toward Norma and could see a part of the prison behind her and began clicking the camera. Then he said, "How about taking your coat off? I would like for your nurse's uniform to be seen in the picture."

Milton had followed Norma and he helped her out of her coat and held it while James took several more pictures. Then he spoke up, "I believe. that is enough pictures, Miss Fleming. It is time for you to go to work, isn't it?"

"You are right. Glad I could help you Mr…UH. I am sorry, but I have forgotten your name."

"That is okay. It's James Webb. We just had that brief meeting at your hardware store on our first day here."

"That is right. I remember you told me all about you and your brother taking pictures of celebrities at government instillations in Florida."

"We certainly haven't seen anyone famous here. However, I don't remember taking the picture of any lady prettier than you Miss Fleming, and I have been taking pictures of beautiful ladies for over ten years. You are so very pretty; I am sure every single man in this place is begging you to marry him."

Norma laughed and put her coat back on. "Mr. Webb, you are flirting with me. Don't waste your time. I am engaged to a wonderful Navy Lt. and will be moving away and getting married as soon as he gets home from somewhere in the Pacific."

"My bad luck but thank you for the pictures." The photographer nodded to Milton and moved away. He crossed the street, got back in the car and drove away.

Milton got in his truck and drove back to the farm. When he got home, he talked to his wife about seeing Norma and the strange man trying to take pictures in front of the prison. Norma spent several minutes after she entered the hospital telling Brandt about the men who were outside the prison taking pictures of people coming and going. Neither of them realized that James Webb had used a telephoto lens to take pictures of the main gate, inside gate and watch towers of the prison as well as the areas surrounding the prison.

Back at the car, James had told his brother that he had finally gotten close-up pictures of the main gate. He reminded John they now had pictures of every one of the watch towers of the prison, every street in Aliceville, and every road leading away from Aliceville. Also, pictures of road sign numbers and signs identifying the distance to the places where each road would lead. The railroad tracks had been photographed, the trains as well as the time each regularly passed through Aliceville. He confided that if they did not get to talk to any prisoners the next day, they would have to return to Panama City. They had been away from their business as long as they could afford.

John agreed but knew he had enjoyed the quiet small town and the very gracious people they had met during their time here.

CHAPTER 19

Brandt thought about the men that Norma had described who were taking pictures outside of the prison. The following morning, he rose and dressed as if he were going to work. He did not enter the hospital but waited by the entry door for Braun to pass on his way to meet Milton Bowen. "Braun, look for that couple of men hanging around outside. Speak to them in German and if they answer listen carefully to every word, they say to repeat to me when you return," Brandt spoke softly.

Braun heard every word Brandt said and nodded to him before he left. Once outside he didn't see anyone but Milton. He hurried to the truck and thanked his lucky stars that the men were not anywhere around. However, they were there when Milton returned him to the prison. Brant quickly got out of the truck because Milton had to hurry on the way to Carrollton to pick up one of his daughters from the Greyhound Bus station. Braun waved goodbye to Milton and headed toward the main gate.

This was the opportunity the two men had been looking for. One of the men approached Braun and spoke in German, "Do you speak German friend?"

"Certainly. All the prisoners here speak German. I see you speak German too. Are you an American?"

"No, I am German but rarely speak German here in the United State. I had hoped for a chance to speak to one of you and inquire about the poor treatment you are receiving from your captors."

"We have been treated very well. No one wants to be kept in prison, but we have adequate food, bed, exercise, and entertainment. We are not interrogated or tortured and there is a hospital where we receive treatment for illness or accidents. Possibly, the information we receive about the war is slanted in favor of the United States and the Allies, but I doubt it."

"I have taken pictures that would be helpful to anyone who escapes these walls and needs help getting out of the United States. I can leave this information at any place you suggest. I also will tell you that my brother and I have a photography shop in Panama City, Florida where we could hide anyone and help them get to New Orleans where our contacts can lead them to safety in South America."

"I will get this information to the prison leaders. I will probably have any message they send you back by tomorrow morning," Braun answered as he entered the front gate.

Once inside Braun went straight to the hospital and looked for Brandt. When he didn't see Brandt, he complained of a severe headache and nausea hoping to stay at the hospital until Brandt arrived. He was given a couple of aspirins and told to go back to his compound. Unsure of what to do, he almost went to headquarters, but decided instead to seek out the prisoner selected to represent all the prisoners, Sgt. Major Walter Meier.

On the way back to his barracks he met Brandt and told him that he was headed to see Sgt. Meier about the conversation he had in German with the man at the gate. Brandt listened carefully and then said, also in German. "I believe you were talking to a German spy, who will most likely get you or anyone of the other prisoners killed. I will go with you to talk to Sgt. Major Meier, and we will determine how to handle this. You may have to make contact with those men tomorrow before you leave for the farm. Meier may have a good suggestion of how to respond to the spy."

After the meeting with Meier and Brandt, Braun was not happy to be the one to give information to the spy, but he had no idea how to refuse to do whatever Sgt. Major Meier requested of him. He left and went straight to his barracks and talked to no one there about the man he had seen near the main gate or his meeting to plan a response.

As he was walking toward the gate the following morning, Brandt was suddenly walking with him and handed him a envelope and said, "Please give this letter to the man as soon as you see him. Do not wait for him to read it; just go to the truck picking you up. Braun, do not speak to him at all. Do you have any questions?"

"No. I hope this is the last time I am involved with these men. Are they Gestapo?"

"I don't think so, but I am not sure. You heard Sgt. Major Meier say he does not believe we will benefit from getting involved with their schemes and some or many prisoners could be killed. Living out the rest of the war here is preferable to escaping here in the middle of the country without money, clothes, or transportation, and the positive relationship we are developing with the Americans is invaluable to us," Brandt explained.

Braun was relieved that he had only one final requirement relating to the man at the gate. He stopped long enough to slip the envelope in his shoe before he reported to the gate for checkout. When he stepped through the gate he saw both Milton's truck and the German man standing some distance behind it He walked slowly toward the truck and dropped down to appear to retie his shoe. He left the envelope on the ground before he got up and got into the truck. He knew the man saw where he left the message because he saw the man wave as the truck drove away.

James Webb went immediately to the envelope left on the ground and hurried to his car with it where his partner was waiting. He opened the letter written in German and read it to John.

> *"The suggestion you sent will not be considered. There have been attempts to escape already and none have been successful. Please leave and do not return. We remain true to the fatherland but will not unnecessarily risk lives that will not impact the war effort."*

"That was short and sweet. These men are soft and don't deserve to be in the army. I am not sure we should have even made the trip up here. We appear to have wasted our gas rations and cash on a hopeless cause," James said.

"I agree. We are packed and ready to leave so we should just return to Panama City and look for another opportunity to sabotage the war effort somewhere along the coast," answered John.

They drove away and never returned to Aliceville or any other of the many prison camps spread across the United States.

CHAPTER 20

August was the month in Aliceville every year when the citizens generally just tried to survive the heat. The several churches in town usually had revival meetings which were well attended, and the movie theater was one of the only air-conditioned buildings in town, so it was usually full no matter what film was showing. Saturday was the day when all the kids in town flocked to see the current serial and the latest cowboy movie. Beyond those events the adults drank lots of sweet tea and sat on the front porch until it was time for bed and the children played kickball or roller skated in the street. Push lawn mowers could be heard in the early morning or after work. Some of the prisoners at the camp looked for shade outside as they wrote letters to be sent to families back in Germany. Even a light rain was a welcome event for everyone.

Norma made sure her mother's yard and flowers were watered and occasionally visited her friend Connie, and always enjoyed her two little boys who seemed to be growing like weeds. Their dad, Larry, was always rolling balls to the boys in the back yard when he got home from work. Norma never questioned why Connie's husband had avoided the war, but sometimes seeing her friends together made her miss Frank even more. Aften several weeks passed with no letters coming, she would find herself becoming tense and anxious. All she was allowed to know was that Frank was on a battleship somewhere in the Pacific. On two occasions she had called Frank's sister Allison in Nashville asking if she or other members of Frank's family had heard from him. Allison's answer had always been no, but she was reassuring and always told Norma that she was sure a letter was on the way. Allison had even called once and invited Norma to come to Nashville during her vacation. Norma had thanked her but told her she didn't take any vacation away from her parents, the hardware store, the farm, or her nursing job at the prison camp.

One afternoon in early September, she found two letters in the mailbox from Frank. She settled down on the front porch with her sweet tea to read both letters when her mother called to her that there was a phone call for her from Nashville. She hurried inside to take the call. She was surprised to hear Frank's sister say, "Hello, Norma, this is Allison Williams. I am so sorry to call you with some very bad news. I am so glad your mother is there with you."

"What is it? I just received two letters from Frank but haven't had a chance to read them yet."

Allison began crying. "Norma, my parents just received a telegram from Washington telling them Frank's ship was sunk by Japanese torpedoes and there are no survivors."

"OH, dear God, no." Norma began crying and suddenly felt her mother's arm around her. She somehow managed to say to Allison, "Thank you for calling me. I will call you back when I get myself together. I can't talk now."

She hung up the phone, collapsed into the kitchen chair and sobbed. Her mother sat down beside her and wiped the tears from her own eyes while she patted her daughter's hand. Norma was unaware of how long she had sat there crying until she finally became aware that she heard her father's voice.

She looked up and spoke to her father. "Daddy, Frank's ship went down, and he is gone. His sister just called me. Her parents got a telegram from Washington."

"Your mother just told me. I will call the camp and tell them you are not coming tonight."

"No, I really need to go in. They are already shorthanded. Both doctors in town are experiencing many cases of flu just like the camp hospital and began asking for help from our doctors yesterday. I must concentrate on the needs of others and not be sitting here wallowing in my loss. All of the men on that ship are being mourned by their families just like me, but we all have to keep on working. Think of the families here in Aliceville who have lost sons. All of us must do our part to finish this war and bring all our people home."

"We are so lucky that we haven't gotten a telegram telling us Ben has been captured or is missing," Florence said.

"Well, I will call and say you may be a little late because of events in the Pacific, but you are coming," George said.

Norma got up and went upstairs to get ready to go to the prison hospital. She placed the letters she had received on her dresser to read later. She couldn't cry any more tonight.

She arrived at work only a few minutes late and saw the hospital was quite busy. Brandt was busy but smiled when he saw her and came over to her and said, "The military doctors have gone to town. The two local doctors were both up all last night and have been working all day. They both called and asked for help. You know they are older men and must get some rest if this epidemic continues for much longer. The senior camp doctor told me to call the German doctors to come in tonight. I have not done so because I have been busy. I expect they will take their time in coming, and I imagine we will need them more tomorrow than tonight. We only have ten flu patients left in the hospital tonight, along with one diabetic, one surgery patient, and one possible heart attack."

Before she even saw her first patient, the hospital door opened, and an obviously very sick prisoner was helped in. Another prisoner and a guard were holding the sick man under his arms. They placed him on the closest empty bed and bolted out. This new patient was rolling in pain. Nurse Fleming began to ask him questions which he did not answer. She called Brandt over because she thought he might not understand English. Brandt questioned him in German, but he blurted out in English, "Don't ask questions! I am hurting. Can't you help me? You should know how bad I am hurting!!!"

"I cannot give you pain medicine without knowing if you have allergies. Do you have allergies? How many hours has it been since you ate?" Nurse Fleming asked.

When he groaned again and twisted, but did not answer, Brandt began a physical examination. "He has very low blood pressure, a very high heart rate, and look at his swollen stomach. He also has an extremely tender abdomen. Brandt looked at Norma and said, "He is in shock. He has an acute abdomen and might have a perforation of a stomach ulcer. He must have surgery now."

"Is one of the German doctors a surgeon?" Norma asked.

"I don't know but it doesn't matter. He is almost dead and will die if he does not have surgery right now. I will do it," answered Brandt.

"You are not a surgeon," Norma said.

"I have assisted in many operations in Berlin and have memorized each step. You will assist me and we can save this man's life."

Norma saw the confidence in Brandt's eyes and began helping him move the patient in the direction of the operation room. The events of the day had so taken her energy and left her dazed, she was not in a position to argue. Once he was on the operating table Brandt began scrubbing to operate while telling Norma which tools needed to be assembled for the surgery. As soon as Brandt came over to the patient, Norma watched him put the patient under anesthesia and begin to perform surgery with care and precision.

When the surgery was over, Brandt thanked Norma for assisting him, but before returning to the main floor of the hospital, he helped Norma move the patient to the recovery room and asked her to stay with him until he awoke and was able to speak.

As Norma sat by the patient, she thought about this special day. Life and death were an everyday part of the war as well as the profession she had chosen. She took pride in Frank and her brother as well as her chosen profession. Nevertheless, she knew the surgery tonight was going to cause much inquiry and might mean she would be fired or might even lose her license as well.

When the patient began moving and opened his eyes, Norma said, "I am Nurse Fleming. Do you remember coming to the hospital?"

"I think so. I suddenly was in a lot of pain. I had been having some stomach pains every day or so, but they usually went away, and I didn't think it was important. Did I come on my own?"

"No, two men brought you, but we didn't even get your name. They just dropped you off and left," Norma answered.

"I am Manfred Mayer. I am in Compound C."

"You are a very lucky man Manfred. You had a perforated stomach ulcer and would have died if you had not come to the hospital and undergone emergency surgery. Are you in any pain now?"

"I feel some pain, but I can handle it."

"That is not necessary. I will go and get some medicine for you," Norma rose from her chair patted Manfred's shoulder and left the recovery room. She found Brandt and told him their patient's name and said she had spoken to him. Brant went immediately to the recovery room to see Manfred himself while Norma went for the pain medicine.

After a brief conversation, Brandt rolled Manfred into a ward and got him settled. He explained that Manfred would be kept in the hospital for about ten days and would be on pain medicine. One reason he would be in the hospital so long was to make sure he didn't get an infection. When Norma came in with the pain medicine, Manfred took it quickly and Norma and Brandt both left, but each checked on him hourly.

A new patient appeared just before Brandt was going off duty. Brandt recognized the usual flu symptoms and took his temperature and blood pressure, but his replacement showed up and took over so Brandt could head to the door. He caught up to Norma just outside the hospital and told her that he would report to Headquarters early in the morning to take responsibility for the surgery.

"I need to be there as well. With no doctor in the hospital, I was the one who should have made the decisions. The fact that you saved that man's life has to count for something," Norma said.

"I made it very clear that Manfred was going to die if the surgery was not done immediately. I gave you no other option. I expect the military doctors will be informed as soon as they arrive back to the camp, and I want to talk to Col. Prince before they do. Please trust me to handle this situation. I am sure you will be asked to make a statement and be asked questions but hopefully that will just be routine," Brandt responded.

"Brandt, I am too exhausted to even think straight tonight. I got a phone call before coming to work from my fiancé's sister that his ship was sunk by Japanese torpedoes somewhere in the Pacific. I think I have been almost comatose since that phone call."

"I am so very sorry. I certainly hope your fiancé somehow survived."

"I can't talk about it anymore. Goodnight," Norma said as she walked slowly through the gates and headed to her car. She knew there were two letters waiting to be read when she got home, and she wasn't sure how she could do it.

CHAPTER 21

Norma's mother had been waiting up for her. She rose from the sofa when she heard Norma open the front door and rushed to her daughter. "Baby, are you okay? I knew I would not go to sleep until you got home."

Mother, you should not have waited for me. You need your rest. I am so sorry that I was such a wreck when Allison called. I still can hardly believe Frank's ship went down. My whole world has become being Frank's wife and now............ I don't know what to do or say."

"Allison called again about two hours after you left. I told her you would call her tomorrow. She just wanted to know that you were all right. She said Frank's mother is in denial and she, Allison, had called a doctor to come to her apartment to give her mother some medicine. I can't even imagine what that poor woman is going through," Florence said.

"Let's both try to get some sleep now. The military doctors are all working in town tonight because of the flu epidemic and the camp hospital was very difficult for me tonight. Thank God you and Dad had mild cases of the flu. I believe you are still vulnerable to be sick again if you are not very careful, and that means no more waiting up for me to get home."

"I think I can go to sleep now that you are safely here. Your father tried to stay up with me, but he kept falling asleep in his chair until I told him to go on upstairs to bed. You don't have a child and can't understand how parents hurt when their child hurts."

"I know Mother. Come, give me your arm and we will go up together," said Norma.

When Norma went into her bedroom, she saw the two letters from Frank lying on her dresser where she had placed them before she left for work. She looked away and prepared for bed. She told herself she would read them tomorrow.

Tomorrow came early. When Norma opened her eyes, her bedside clock showed it to be 6:20 which was much earlier than she usually awoke. She knew she was not going back to sleep and could not continue to just look at the two letters from Frank, so she took them both from the dresser and climbed back in bed to read them. She first opened the one with the oldest postmark of the two. It was like a typical letter from Frank. She was already crying by just seeing his handwriting, and his words made it worse. He always wrote how much he missed her especially when he had finished his work for the day and was alone in his cabin. He told her about looking out on a beautiful ocean and only occasionally seeing an island in the distance. He never mentioned any battles occurring or seeing any Japanese ships or airplanes. In this letter, he did ask about her parents and said he was hoping to get a letter from her and his sister at the mail call for the day, and always closed with love and long kisses. The second letter was written a few days later. In it he first wrote that he had just received a letter from her and one from his parents but was still hoping for a letter from his sister that would give him details honestly about how his parents were managing their lives and their health. He did mention his roommate who was married and had pictures of his children all over their room. Norma wondered if Frank had a picture of her out in his room, but she knew she would never know the answer to that question. After she finished reading the letter, she got out of bed and placed both of the letters in the box in the back of her closet where she had saved every letter Frank had written to her since he had left to go to California to become a Naval officer.

She was still softly crying when she went on the bathroom to shower and dress for the day. She could not remember any day in her life that she dreaded more than today. It was the first full day that she knew her fiancé was dead, and she had to face the doctors at the camp hospital and confess to the surgery that had occurred last night. She decided she would go by her church and see her pastor before going to the camp this afternoon.

By the time she went downstairs, her parents were sitting at the breakfast table talking quietly. They both looked up when she walked into the kitchen. "Oh, Norma, I had hoped you were still asleep," Florence said.

"Mother, I could say the same to you. I told you last night that you must stay rested, so you stay well, and how are you dad?"

"I slept fine," said George. "I tried to get your mother to go to bed when I did, but she was determined to wait up for you. You know she can be blasted difficult when she wants to be."

"Like you are always easy to get along with!" said Florence.

"Please, you two. Don't fuss with each other. I don't need any more to deal with today. After I get a cup of coffee, I have to call Allison and ask about Frank's parents. They were so proud of him. I know they are distraught," Norma said as she poured herself a cup and took a long drink.

"It is easy to get short with each other when there is trouble, but you don't have to worry about us. We have been together through many hard times before and we will face whatever comes down the road in the future together," said George.

"I know Dad. You two are hard as a rock and help keep me going. I am so glad that I am here with you both since I have lost Frank. I just lost my compass and will be depending on you both to help me navigate these next months," Norma admitted.

"Norma, I know you haven't lost your faith in God. I am glad you are here with us, but our heavenly Father knows of your loss and will comfort you," said Florence.

"I know. I am going by the church on my way to work this afternoon. I meant that having you and Dad right here is so much better than my being in Nashville or anywhere else. You two love me and I love you so very much means I have your help in deciding what I will do after Ben comes home and I must move on with my life. Do you understand? Mother, remember the three of us sitting down and discussing where I would go to nursing school?"

"Yes, I do. We are so lucky to have found such a prestigious nursing school this close to Aliceville."

"It certainly worked well for me, but I doubt that I will want to return there now. I have to call Allison now before it gets any later."

Norma went over to the phone and called the operator to place a call to Allison Williams in Nashville. In a moment she heard Allison speak.

"Hello, this is Norma. I am so sorry I failed to call you back yesterday afternoon, but I was so out of control. I couldn't talk, and when you called back, I had gone to the hospital here because we were overrun with many people coming down with the flu, and we didn't have enough workers."

"I certainly understand. I was just worried about you. My parents and I have been crying since the telegram arrived yesterday. My father has put in a call to a friend he has who works in Naval Intelligence to see if he can get more information about what happened than the brief and abrupt telegram that was sent. If we learn any more details, especially about the possibility of survivors, I will call you again Norma. I personally believe if there was any chance of Frank being alive, the telegram would have only said missing in action. However, I read it and it clearly said there were no survivors."

"Thank you for calling me so promptly. I know we were not officially engaged, but we had decided to get married as soon as he got home. Please tell your parents that my heart is broken for your whole family, and I will call you and come to see all of you at some time in the future. I will hang up now in case your father receives a call from that friend about Frank's ship. Thanks again for letting me know about Frank and please call me if you get further information. Bye now," Norma spoke loudly enough that her parents heard all that she had said to Allison.

Norma hung up the phone, took a deep breath, and turned to face her parents. "Allison's father has a friend who is trying to find out more information about the ship sinking, but it does not appear that there is any chance that Frank might be alive. Dad, you need to go on to the store, Mother, you can just sit there while I clean up the kitchen. We will just have to continue living each day as we have been doing."

CHAPTER 22

Norma left the house early enough to go by her church before she went to work at the base hospital. When she walked into the building the ranking doctor was waiting for her. He spoke to her in a very formal manner. "Nurse Fleming, would you come with me to Headquarters."

"Yes Sir," she answered and followed him out the door and into the Headquarters building. He continued down a hall into what appeared to be a conference room with a long table where a number of officers were seated as well as Sgt. Major Walter Meier and Victor Brandt. The doctor indicated she was to be seated at the end of the table.

"Gentlemen," the doctor still standing began speaking, "This is Nurse Fleming. She was hired as a civilian supplement in this hospital even before I arrived. She trained at Vanderbilt Nursing School located at Vanderbilt Medical School in Nashville, Tennessee. She was an honor student and hired to work at Vanderbilt Hospital immediately after she graduated from her training. The staff here called for a recommendation after she applied to work here and received an excellent recommendation on the phone which was followed up by a written recommendation signed by the chief nurse in the hospital there in Nashville. Her work here has been top notch. Both the military members who have been patients as well as the prisoners who have been patients all have found her to be very capable, kind, and helpful. If she were to leave, I seriously doubt we could replace her with a nurse of her quality at this time. Now, we will begin our discussion of the events of the last evening in which Nurse Fleming took part. Nurse

Fleming, I will now ask you to describe in detail the events that occurred last evening at this hospital."

Norma looked around the table at each person in the room. Most were sitting quietly and looking straight ahead. A few were looking down. Brandt was the only one who looked at her and he winked at her without changing his facial expression. She almost smiled but did not. She began speaking by thanking the doctor for his kind words and then began by noting that she had observed that there were no doctors in the hospital when she arrived at work and realized she was the senior staff member there.

She quickly moved on to her asking the orderly Brandt to explain the absence of the doctors which she reiterated. Then she began talking about the very sick and writhing patient who was carried in by a prisoner and a guard. She told about her attempt to interview him about his condition and his inability to answer questions. She went in depth explaining the examination Brandt began and noted he began pointing out the severity of the patient's condition, and it became obvious that this patient had a serious condition that might be a perforated ulcer and would die if he did not undergo surgery immediately. She recalled that she asked if one of the German doctors who had worked all day was a surgeon. Brandt had answered that he didn't know, but he did know that the patient would die before the German doctors could be wakened, found out if one was a surgeon, and then wait for him to shower before getting dressed and reporting to the operating room. Finally, she recalled Brant telling her that he had observed this surgery many times and knew he could save this patient's life. She explained that she felt pressure to make a life and death decision, and given no other options, she decided to proceed with the surgery. Attempting to help save the prisoner's life was her primary focus. In conclusion, she said she had observed an operation as well done as any she had ever seen, and the patient was out of recovery and in a ward talking in as short a time as she had ever witnessed. Her final words were that she knew that Manfred would be sitting up talking when she got to the hospital that evening. Given this positive outcome she felt like the correct decision had been made.

The doctor had seated himself while she was talking, but now that she had stopped, he again rose and asked the group to ask Nurse Fleming any question that anyone felt they needed answered. It was quiet for about thirty seconds and then the questions began. It didn't take Norma long to realize that these men were not doctors, but were just staff officers assigned to the prison camp. That really surprised her, but she politely answered each question and tried to use layman's language when possible. When all the questions were answered, the doctor thanked all of the men for their attention to details and escorted Norma back to the hospital where he left her. She imagined he had returned to the meeting that was occurring at the Headquarters Building.

She checked on Manfred and found him just as she had suggested he would be. When he saw her, he smiled. She smiled back and went to work doing her job. She thought to herself that at least so far tonight it was still her job and she had helped to save someone's life. The hours passed quickly and when she looked at the wall clock, she realized it was within ten minutes until her replacement would be coming in. She knew she had not thought of Frank since she had left the church before coming to work. It was very clear that work was the best way for her to handle her grief.

When she stepped out of the hospital to head home Brandt was waiting for her. Before she could stop herself, she asked, "Is that meeting finally over?"

"Yes, and I wanted to be the one who told you about what was decided after you left," he answered.

"Well, tell me. I can take it, Brandt."

"First, let me say, I want you to know I was very proud of the way you told those officers about what happened last night as well as how you answered their questions.

"Tell me what will happen next!"

"They decided that this incident was now closed. The German prisoner received a procedure that saved his life, and here in the middle of war life needs to be saved under unusual circumstances quite often. Last evening was one of those occasions. A young man's life was saved even though he was an enemy combatant. I did tell them that I had attended some medical school classes and that satisfied the doctor. I am not sure anyone else realized how close to death Manfred came. If the patient had been an American, they might have sent their findings to a higher authority, but I really doubt it. I think they didn't want to find fault with success, but it was made clear to me that I was not to do anymore procedures unless directed to do so by an American military doctor. I also think not all the doctors will leave the hospital at the same time again no matter what crisis is occurring anywhere in the United States."

"I went to the church before coming to work this afternoon and talked to my minister. He said a prayer that God would help me accept the loss of Frank without being filled with hatred and help me to use the gifts God has given me throughout my life. I was afraid I might lose my license and that would have meant I could no longer be a nurse. Maybe both of us should say a prayer of thanksgiving tonight for God's answered prayers," Norma touched Brandt's arm briefly before she left him standing and walked toward the gate.

Brandt could still feel her touch that had taken his breath away. He finally was able to call out to her, "I will be at work with you tomorrow."

CHAPTER 23

Brandt had difficulty in going to sleep that night. He knew it was not caused by the report he had given to Col. Prince and Lt. Col. William Waite, Col. Prince's upcoming replacement. Both men had listened to his explaining the difficult situation in the hospital that had resulted in his performing surgery. He also knew it was not the meeting Col. Prince set up with a group of men on his staff and the ranking doctor at the camp in which he and Sgt. Major Meier also attended. He also knew it was not the appearance of Nurse Fleming and her detailed description of the hospital that evening and her candid observation of the surgery he had performed and its aftermath. He knew it was not the long discussion the group had in making the decision to make no further report on the incident, but he knew it was the few short moments he had spent with Norma Fleming where she told him her fiancé was lost in the Pacific and her touching his arm.

Brandt knew he had fallen in love with her, but he had not realized how difficult it would be not to take her in his arms and try to relieve some of her pain. He told himself he was not a young man who had never experienced any passion, but even the cold shower he had taken before going to bed had not helped him calm down his feelings. He kept seeing her sad expression, teary eyes, and quivering lips. His current condition seemed hopeless.

Sometime in the early morning hours he fell asleep. When he awoke, his hand was clinched as if holding a scalpel and the events he had experienced in the last two days were what he had been dreaming about. He was concentrated on the surgery, even though it had been several years now since he had actually held a scalpel. Now completely awake and in the light of day, he knew he had not lost his touch when he made the incision. That long time ago when he had made the snap decision to exchange his clothes and identity with the dead soldier, he had not had time to reflect on how he would miss his true profession.

He quickly dressed and headed out for breakfast, but when he looked at the available food he only reached for a cup of coffee. He was unaware of who he had sat down beside him until the person spoke. "You look like you are a million miles away from Aliceville," said his friend Felix Fischer.

"Well, seeing you certainly makes me aware again. I have been very busy these last few days and have not had a chance to ask you how you are doing," said Brandt.

"Since you have now asked, I will tell you that I have been practicing with my soccer team every day. We have gotten quite good and may well become the camp champions. You should come and see us play. You will be very proud because our team's players are all from our barracks. We do have a game scheduled for late afternoon. Why don't you come?"

"That just might be the distraction that I need. The hospital has been totally consuming my mind and body for days now. Have you heard about any of the events that have recently occurred there?" asked Brandt.

"Nothing but idle gossip about an orderly getting way out of line. You have probably been asked to speak to him if that is true," Felix said. "I know you had pretty wise advice when we were on the train coming here and have continued with good advice since then," he added.

"Those are kind words, Felix, and couldn't have come at a better time. Those eggs smell good. I think I will eat breakfast after all," Brandt said.

Brandt did eat eggs, peanut butter toast, and ham! He and Felix talked about soccer and Brandt promised to come to the soccer game that afternoon before he headed to the hospital to work.

Brandt remembered that this whole experience of being in the German Army, the fighting in north Africa, and being captured and interned in a prison in the United States was not all about him and his ego. He remembered he was supposed to be making these thousands of young men not think their lives were over because of being prisoners for a few years in a foreign country. He knew he was helping them accept and survive with what they saw as losing their self-respect. As he walked back toward the barracks, he told himself that he would continue working with Norma in the hospital, but not reveal his feelings for her and certainly wouldn't perform another surgery until he found it necessary to admit he was actually a German officer and surgeon.

CHAPTER 24

Norma had received no phone call from Nashville when she got home from the hospital last night and no call this morning. She had fallen asleep knowing that her job had been saved and her career was not compromised. She knew she would be watched more carefully by her employers for the next few months, but she had really dodged a bullet and a mine field. Now, she just needed to know Frank had somehow survived.

She joined her parents for breakfast and saw them smiling at each other which seemed that everything was back to normal between them. Norma felt like all of her family had weathered a storm and would survive this terrible war. "I was so pleased that you didn't wait up for me again," Norma said to her mother.

"I admit I heard you come in but went back to sleep. I had wanted to hear the phone if it rang, but when you came in, I knew you would hear and I could finally relax," Florence answered.

"No call from Nashville is not good news, but it is still early, and I will not completely give up just yet," Norma said.

"This might be a good time for you to go out to the farm and ride Doll. I can handle the store this morning. The weather is cool," said George as he rose from the table, reached for his old straw hat and headed to the door.

"Thank you, Dad. I will take you up on that. It has been too long since I have been to the farm. It will be nice to see Milton and Wilma, and also Karl Braun."

"Yes, Karl is making himself right at home at the farm. The Bowens family act like he is essential as well. It was very smart of me to ask for Karl to be allowed to work full time at the farm," said George.

"He is lucky that he has avoided getting the flu that is all over Pickens County and the prison camp," said Norma. "I think those photographers that were here a while ago took pictures of Karl and me, but Milton was adamant about not waiting for them to take his picture. I never understood that."

"You can ask him while you are at the farm today," said George as he waved goodbye and shut the door.

Norma left soon after and arrived at the farm while it was still early. She sat and visited with Wilma until Milton returned from the prison camp with Karl Braun. She headed to the barn and when Braun saw her wearing slacks, he hurried into the barn and began to saddle Doll. When Norma saw what he was doing she said, "Braun, saddle that other old horse and ride with me."

"Thank you, Nurse Fleming. It is not often I talk to a woman," he answered as he brought out Buster and began to saddle him.

The two of them rode around the perimeter of the farm and discussed which fields would be planted the following year and which one would be left fallow. Norma also pointed to places where the fence was beginning to sag and needed some support. After a thorough inspection of the entire farm they returned the horses to the barn where both horses received a rub down followed by a generous handful of grain.

Before leaving the barn, Norma thanked Braun for the work he was doing at the farm with little or no supervision. She realized suddenly that her anger for the war was raging against the Japanese since the death of Frank, but at least for the German prisoners at the Aliceville camp she felt some compassion.

Before Norma drove back home, she remembered to mention to Milton and ask why he had insisted that the visiting photographers not take his picture and not take a picture of him with Braun outside the prison. He explained he did not know who the two men were and was afraid he would somehow be accused of mistreating a German prisoner which he was certainly not doing. Norma knew she would never have thought of the possibility of that complication. There were people who could possibly misinterpret how the prisoners at Aliceville were involved in the community. She prayed people everywhere knew the prisoners were peacefully contributing to the economy in Aliceville, Pickens County, and throughout the state of Alabama.

As she drove home, Norma thought about her animosity toward the Japanese who had attacked Pearl Harbor and started this awful war, and her conflicting feelings about the Germans she was working with at the hospital or were her patients. She hoped this war could end by the end of 1943, but that was not to be.

CHAPTER 25

Norma and Brandt showed up to work at the hospital that afternoon. Norma looked tired but appeared to be in control of her emotions. Brandt was pleased to see her going about her work without hesitation and confidently. They smiled briefly and only spoke about the patients they were working with. Only after their shift had ended did Brandt finally ask, "Have you gotten anymore news about what happened in the Pacific?"

"No," she said and after a moment added, "I have not lost hope, but I am trying to be realistic."

"I am so sorry. I wish I had the words to relieve your fears, but I know you are strong enough to accept this possible loss and continue to fulfill the work you are doing here to relieve suffering."

Norma did not answer, but just quietly nodded her head and left the hospital. Brandt watched her leave and wanted to follow her, but told himself that would not be appropriate, so he just left and headed toward the canteen where he heard the prison's band playing music. He hoped the noise and activity there would be engaging because he did not think he was ready to go back to the barracks and lie in bed thinking about Norma.

One of the first prisoners he saw was Karl Braun. Karl saw him at the same time and motioned for Brandt to join him at his table. Both men exchanged pleasantries and then Braun said, "Nurse Fleming came to the farm this morning, and we both rode horses all around the farm. She shared with me the plans for next planting season and showed me which fields we were leaving fallow. She showed me several spots on the fence that were sagging where a person or animal might get cut on the barbed wire that I am to repair, and she told me about some other work she wanted me to do over the next weeks. She is well informed about a working farm and a very nice person."

Brandt's jaw tightened and he thought to himself that he came here to keep from thinking about Norma, and the first person he talked to immediately spoke about her. Not only spoke about her, but implied they had a long conversation which he had enjoyed. Norma had barely spoken to him, but she had easily talked and shared plans with Braun while they were both enjoying a horseback ride. He realized he was very jealous of Braun!

"Does she come to the farm often to ride horses with you?"

"Today was the very first time, but I hope she comes again. It was the first time I have really talked to her since the interview before I went to work on her family's farm. It was very nice to talk to a woman about the farm instead of only talking about this bloody war and living in a prison camp."

"I am sure that is true. By the way, do you have a girlfriend back in Germany? Brandt asked.

"I knew several girls, but I was not walking out with a special one. I have not written to anyone but my mother since I have been here."

"I believe Nurse Fleming is quite a few years older than you, and I think she has a fiancé in the U.S. Navy," Brandt said, knowing he couldn't help providing these facts.

Braun nodded his head indicating he understood, and changed the subject to the band that was playing, "Chattanooga Choo Choo." "I like the beat of this American music, but those words are not ones I have heard at anytime or anyplace and I have been learning many new English words," he confided.

"I believe those words are pure American. I never heard them in England when I visited there when I was a young man. You have figured out from the words that Chattanooga is a city in another state and choo choo is the sound a train makes. Right?" Brandt responded.

"Yes, but I will not tell anyone in Germany that I rode on a choo choo in the United States!" Brandt answered and both men laughed.

Their laughter relieved the tension that Brandt was feeling and both men continued talking until Brandt found himself yawning and felt like he was relaxed enough that he could go to sleep. He told Braun goodnight and left the canteen. He found himself humming "Chattanooga Choo Choo" all the way to his barracks. He slipped quietly into his bed and wondered how a country, where a song about a choo choo was so popular among adults, was very possibly winning a war against the Axis Powers.

CHAPTER 26

Mail had been arriving at Aliceville Prison Camp since about two months after the first prisoners arrived. The Red Cross wanted the German people to know about the treatment the prisoners were receiving. Meier had been assigned to sign for all mail that arrived for the prisoners. He was careful to see that if the mail was for individual prisoners, it was promptly delivered. Up until this time Victor Brandt had written no letters and received no mail. He certainly had not expected any.

This meant Brandt was not expecting to be woken the following morning by receiving a letter clearly address to Victor Brandt. He was startled. He wondered how anyone in Germany had figured out to write Brandt in Aliceville. Even if he had been reported as missing, there were numerous internment camps in all of the Allies countries. He took a deep breath and slit open the letter. The first place he looked in the single page letter was the closing and the signature. It read, "With love, Sophia."

He prayed before he began reading that Sophia was not Brandt's wife. He felt somewhat relieved as he carefully read the short letter. Sophia identified herself as Brandt's sister who was writing to tell him that she was alive and had moved out of the city into the countryside. She said she was now living at their cousin's farm in Bavaria where they had visited before the war. She ended the letter with confirming that there was no one else to tell that she was alive and where she could be found. Certainly, Brandt was relieved that Sophia was not a wife, but sorry this woman was making a desperate attempt to reach her only brother who was supposed to be a prisoner of war in faraway America. He realized the war was causing much pain and suffering to the civilians on both sides.

That evening when Norma came in, he saw in her face that she had not received any good news about her fiancé. He had decided last night that he would confront her about her horseback riding with Karl, but after reading the letter from Sophia he decided to keep quiet. Women on both sides were victims of this war. Instead, he said, "Good Evening, Nurse Fleming. I hope it is not to forward to say, you look lovely this evening."

"Thank you, Brandt. I am feeling better," she answered.

"Braun told me that you got to go horseback riding yesterday," he said and wanted to kick himself for mentioning the horseback riding when he had just told himself he would not mention it!

"Yes, I have had Doll since I was sixteen, and I always enjoy riding, especially on a lovely fall day like yesterday."

"I enjoy riding too. Maybe, someday I can go with you."

"I am glad to hear that. I will see if that can be arranged," Norma replied.

As a doctor approached Norma's back, Brandt said, "Yes, this patient's temperature has been normal for the last several hours and he has kept his last meal down."

"That is good news. He appears to be recovering. Nurse Fleming, if he continues on this path, I expect he will not need any medication tonight," said the doctor as he walked by Norma and Brandt.

When the doctor was out of earshot, Norma said, "I am glad you saw him approaching us."

"I knew he didn't need to hear us having a personal conversation so soon after our "event," Brandt said.

Both nurse and orderly smiled at each other and moved in two different directions. They were soon so busy that they didn't have another personal moment until their shifts were over. Brandt spoke first, "I received a letter today from Germany."

"I know letters are coming for the prisoners," Norma answered.

"I certainly didn't expect a letter," Brandt said.

"Did your family know you were in North Africa? Maybe the army notified the Red Cross the names of all the men who were taken prisoner there," Norma said. "Who was the letter from?"

"Sophia," answered Brandt.

"Is she someone special to you?"

"Oh no, I mean she is special because she is a sister, not a girlfriend or anything like that," Brandt answered.

"I am glad you got a letter from home. I hope she sent good news to you," Norma said.

"She has left Berlin and is living on a farm in Bavaria," Brandt said and added, "It is probably safer there than in a city."

"I know you are happy she is alive. Did she mention your parents?" Norma asked.

Brandt did not know how to best answer that question. He had no idea about Brandt's parents, so after a pause he only said, "No."

Norma recognized his reluctance to answer about his parents. She decided to change the subject. "By the way, did you notice that a number of prisoners were leaving the camp this morning? Just like the group that left several weeks ago; the guard at the gate told me they were being sent to Camp Alva in Oklahoma."

"That does not surprise me. The Americans are attempting to segregate the hard-core Nazi population from the rest of the prisoners. You remember the prisoner with the broken arm who also lost sight in one eye after the fight in the barracks, don't you? He was attacked for making a very positive statement about the treatment we are receiving here in Aliceville. Those kinds of attacks are continuing, as wells as, one group of prisoners were pretending to be soldiers who were actually officers. All of these are examples of disruptive behavior and cannot be tolerated by the commander," Brandt explained.

"Please be careful that you don't get caught up in a disagreement that escalates into fighting. I certainly don't want you to become a victim or even injured," Norma answered.

"Don't you worry. I like being in the hospital working with you, but never want to be a patient," Brandt said.

He took hold of one of Norma's hands and held it while looking into her eyes. She looked back just as intently and smiled. Brandt raised the hand holding her hand to his face and kissed her hand. Her smile slowly disappeared, but she did not jerk her hand away.

When he finally released her hand no words passed between them, but they parted and headed in two different directions. Norma went to the gate and her car and Brandt to the canteen looking for Braun or Fischer, his best friends.

CHAPTER 27

Norma drove away from the prison camp, but she did not drive home. Instead, she drove downtown and parked in front of the Fleming Hardware store. She used her key to enter the store and went to the back into the office. She wanted to be by herself for a while. She sat at the old desk while she tried to relax and let her mind search her feelings about all of the things that had been happening in her life over the last weeks. She knew she had truly loved Frank, or at least she thought she had loved him. The war had disrupted their lives and both of them had made very important life decisions without consulting the other. She knew her parents would not have done that. She knew if a marriage truly worked that both partners had to work together as a team. She also knew that Frank was more than likely dead now, and she would have to accept that reality before she could move forward with her life. Only if Frank was alive, could the two of them discuss the importance of becoming a team and being the loving couple, she knew they both wanted.

At the same time, she was very concerned about the feelings that she knew she was developing with Victor Brandt. They worked closely together every day. They carefully listened to each other and arrived at decisions together. They had jointly decided to operate on a dying man in order to save his life without any regard for how destructive that decision might be to their lives and how that decision might jeopardize their futures. She had truly enjoyed their intimate moment just prior to her leaving the hospital grounds, and she had felt so guilty that she knew she wasn't in a frame of mind to just go home. How could she, a very level-headed person, become a free spirit who could fall in love with a German prisoner who would be returning to Germany after the war ended?

Norma knew her world was in turmoil. She finally realized there were no easy answers she could arrive at tonight, so she reluctantly left the store and went home. She hoped she would awake tomorrow without feeling so much confusion, but she knew that was unlikely. She entered as quietly as possible and headed upstairs to her bedroom. Lying on her dresser was a letter from Frank's sister Allison. It had obviously come today, and her mom or dad had brought it upstairs so she would find it when she got home. She stared at it for a long time before picking it up and opening it. She read it slowly and it said exactly what she had known it would say when she first saw it.

Allison wrote that her dad's friend had talked to his friends who were high ranking Navy and Army men who had verified that there were no survivors when Frank's battleship was sunk by the Japanese torpedoes. Allison said she couldn't call Norma again without crying, but knew Norma was waiting for any news that she had found out and had to be told. She said her parents were very broken up, and they were now in the process of cleaning out Frank's apartment and deciding what to do with his car before they returned to their home.

Norma folded the letter and put it back in the envelope and placed it back on her dresser. She wanted to put it in the box with his letters, but it didn't seem to belong there. She decided she would take it downstairs for her parents to read when she left for work tomorrow. Perhaps that would be the easiest way to get past having to tell them that Frank was not going to be coming home. She lay in bed staring at the ceiling but did not cry. She was all cried out.

When she returned to work the following day, even more prisoners were being moved out of Aliceville. Some of this group she had seen in the hospital recently. Brandt told her that these were troublemakers being sent to a prison camp somewhere in Florida. He added, "Don't worry Norma. There will still be plenty of prisoners left here to keep both of us busy. Already today we have seven patients complaining of sore throats and fever."

After running several tests the doctors determined these sick prisoners were suffering from diphtheria. Since diphtheria can be a fatal disease, all six thousand people, both German prisoners and American military and civilians, at the camp had to be tested for immunity. More than twelve hundred proved to be unvaccinated or vulnerable for getting the disease. The American doctors joined by the German doctors immediately began an immunization program. Both Norma and Brandt spent time working with many prisoners who were afraid of the shot and insisted they had already been vaccinated upon entering the army. Brandt told each one of these that he had worked in German military hospitals and knew that was not true. When Norma was unable to convince a stubborn prisoner, she called Brandt who lost no time in changing the prisoner's mind.

Following the diphtheria challenge that lasted for over a period of several weeks, Norma and Brandt finally were able to have another personal moment together. "I have really missed getting to talk to you," Brandt said.

"Yes, so have I," Norma said.

"How are your parents?"

"They are about the same. They both dread the weather getting colder and miss Ben. He has written that he cannot be home for Thanksgiving which I expected. We will probably go to the farm and be with the Bowens and their two daughters for the holiday," Norma said.

"That is a holiday that we Germans do not celebrate. It is about a meal that early settlers had with Indians, isn't it?" asked Brandt.

"Yes. The Pilgrims in Massachusetts celebrated their first harvest in the new world. They invited the Indians to the feast because they had helped make the harvest possible. Mostly it is a time to overeat and attend a local football game or listen to a game on the radio," Norma said.

"That sure sounds like fun to me," Brandt admitted.

"Brandt, you sound just like a typical American man!"

"No Norma, that is just a typical man!"

Thanksgiving Day 1943 came just like a typical American holiday with the only exception being thousands and thousands of American army, navy, marines, and coast guard members were not home with their families and there were no football games. The war had meant no games would be played until the war ended.

CHAPTER 28

The prisoners celebrated All Souls' Day late on November 2nd. Each compound was allowed to have a parade and celebrate for an hour because this was a Roman Catholic Church Feast Day always celebrated in Germany. The prisoners announced they held the parade to honor their fallen heroes.

This event was followed by Meier distributing a sheet of general announcements through all the compounds. It listed cultural, sports, educational and religious activities. It was not a newspaper, but Meier worked for the next nine months to get a printing press and was able to finally print a camp newspaper toward the end of 1944.

Now in late 1943, the camp continued to improve in many different ways. Besides each compound having its own recreation area, a general recreation area had been constructed where compounds competed against each other. Even boxing matches were held. The camp school had grown from English classes to courses in arithmetic, art, drawing, history, mathematics, painting, pottery, woodworking, and several other languages. The library had a collection of books and newspapers. The camp chapel had a prisoner chaplain and two American army chaplains. Every service held had good attendance.

The one area where there was a concern was the lack of enough winter clothing. With over five thousand prisoners, as well as, the German doctors and one German chaplain there was a shortage of overcoats and raincoats as the winter weather was moving into Alabama. Norma and Brandt began quizzing patients about the winter clothing they had or had not received. Norma took the need for winter sweaters that could be worn under the prisoners PW shirts to all the churches in town and collected several hundred sweaters which she brought to the hospital in several boxes. She gave them to Brandt and he recruited several American guards to help him deliver the boxes to Meier for distribution.

When Brandt returned from delivering the sweaters to Meier he said, "Norma, the people here in Aliceville are very generous to give that many sweaters to us."

"The Bible says if you are being asked for your coat, you should give your cloak as well," Norma answered. "We have a lot of good Christian people here in Aliceville."

"I certainly agree with you. Meier insisted I keep this very nice sweater for myself," Brandt said.

"I am so glad. I put in a couple of my brother Ben's sweaters and even one from my father's, but the one you got came from someone at the Baptist Church I think," Norma answered.

"Meier picked it for me. It is in good shape and I probably would have not chosen it, but would have selected one that looked more worn. I will trade it with someone who is wearing one with a hole or other flaw," Brandt stated.

"Don't do that Brandt. Meier is aware that you are working here in the hospital as well as helping any prisoner who needs help for any reason. I think he was trying to thank you for all you do to help him and all of the prisoners here," Norma insisted.

"That is kind of you Norma. I hope I have helped anyone who comes to me or is sent to me for help. Being here could make some people aggressive or suicidal. Neither of those attitudes will help anyone survive this imprisonment," Brandt answered.

"I hope any Americans who are imprisoned by the Germans or the Japanese have someone who is helping them survive being a prisoner of war," Norma said.

"I do to Norma, and I hope that every sick or injured prisoner, has a nurse who is as kind, loving and as competent as you are," he added.

"Okay, Brandt, that is enough complimenting each other!"

"Well, if we don't compliment each other, I am not sure we will get any kind words."

Both laughed and suddenly were hugging each other. Just as suddenly they realized they were locked in an embrace, and they immediately broke apart. Norma looked at Brandt and realized she was blushing.

"No need to blush, you have done nothing wrong Norma."

"There are over one hundred patients in this hospital tonight and we need to get busy," Norma said as she moved toward the first patient that needed attention. Brandt followed her lead and they both worked tirelessly for the entire shift. When it was time to leave Brandt opened the door for both of them and outside they both waved goodbye and headed in the same opposite directions that they took after every night's work.

CHAPTER 29

By December 1944 the lives of the German prisoners at Camp Aliceville continued to improve, but the war news in the American newspapers and the American newsreels at the movies were presenting a different picture to the Aliceville citizens. The Americans began to show progress in moving toward Germany. The Germans were losing their holdings in Russia and even Berlin was now being bombed by the British. Brandt listened to the American doctors discuss what they were hearing about the war. He knew the German Army as well as the Japanese were suffering defeat after defeat.

The German prisoners here in Aliceville were unaware of what reverses the Axis Powers were experiencing and were preparing for Christmas. They had created an orchestra that sounded so professional that they were invited to play at the Officers' Club where their music was enjoyed by the American officers and their wives. The single officers were often accompanied by the local girls they had met. Occasionally, Brandt quietly slipped in and watched the dancing. He imagined holding Norma in his arms gliding around the dance floor. One Saturday evening he was surprised to see Norma sitting at a table with one of the American doctors and his wife. He was shocked when she even danced with the doctor while his wife sat there smiling. She appeared to be an accomplished dancer. Brandt kept learning more about Norma's many diverse interests and abilities.

The first chance he got the following Monday he asked her about being at the Officers' Club. She responded that the doctor had insisted she come with him and his wife. Norma asked him, "How did you know I was there?"

"I heard the music as I was leaving the hospital, and looked in to see if it were the prisoners' orchestra playing and when I looked around the room, I saw you. Those prisoners are really good musicians and you certainly seemed to be enjoying the evening."

"I think the doctor knows this Christmas will be very hard for me and was wanting me to have a short time to forget about Frank dying."

"He seems to be a very kind man. I am glad he thought of a way to help you. Even during this war most people are thinking only of their own family and friends," Brandt said. "This is one of the times, I wish I was free to spend more time with you."

"Brandt, I know we are on opposite sides in this war, but we both know we have become friends. No matter, what the future holds, I believe our friendship will survive," Norma said.

"On Christmas Eve my Compound, Compound A, is presenting Bach's Christmas Oratorio. It will be in German, but I believe you will enjoy the music and singing. I have no way to give you a Christmas gift except to offer this program for you. I am actually singing in the chorus and would so like for you to be in the audience," Brandt said.

Norma, reached out and took Brandt's hand, "I will most certainly be there. That is a wonderful program for your compound to undertake. I had no idea you were a singer. Are you a tenor or a bass?"

"I am probably a baritone, but I am singing bass in this program. Most of the young men in the compound sing tenor. You will be surprised at how good the voices are, especially the ones who are singing the solos."

"My church has their program the Sunday before Christmas and also on Christmas Day, so Christmas Eve is a perfect time for me to come here. Thank you for inviting me."

"Thank you for coming," said Brandt as he gazed into her eyes.

Norma knew the meaning of the Christmas season. The beautiful lights, the decorations, the music and singing all contributed to making everyone more caring, but she knew her feelings for Brandt were not dependent on the holiday season.

CHAPTER 30

In 1944 many changes occurred at the Aliceville Internment Camp. Most of the earliest camps built in the United States had been put in relatively remote areas for security reasons, as was Aliceville. However, as the war continued more and more Americans were drafted or decided to join the military. This meant there was a growing need for many more workers to keep the American economy at the high level needed to support the war. Thousands of women entered the workforce and it became necessary to move many of the prisoners to areas where there were more working opportunities for them.

Suddenly in the middle of January a thousand prisoners were moved from Aliceville to Fort Dix in New Jersey. Norma and Brandt both stood together outside the hospital along with a large group of other hospital workers watching the prisoners march out of the camp headed to the train and the trip north. Some of these men had been patients and Norma was surprised she actually remembered several of their names. She suspected she would never see them again. Brandt remembered some prisoners from the ship that had brought them from North Africa and remembered their insecurity and dread of coming to the United States. It was a moment of recognition that they were all without any control of their lives and at the mercy of the war effort.

"How did they decide which prisoners to move?" Norma asked the doctor standing next to her.

"I am not sure, but I imagine the German NCO in each barracks must have listed the prisoners who would be most willing to work. I understand there are many jobs in the New Jersey area that would be glad to take willing workers. There is simply not enough work in this area," the doctor answered.

Brandt had heard Norma's question and the doctor's answer. "There are some prisoners here who refuse to work. It would serve no purpose to send them. The NCO in each barracks knows who will be cooperative and will keep the noncompliant ones here," Brandt added.

"Those are the very ones I would want to be rid of," said Norma.

"I didn't mean they are belligerent, if anything they are loyal Germans who are unwilling to help the Allies." Brandt explained.

"I doubt the ones who are leaving will receive better treatment in New Jersey than they have received here in Aliceville. I hope the Germans are treating American prisoners as well as we are treating their prisoners," Norma said.

"I rather doubt our boys are receiving the health care we are providing," the doctor said.

"I pray you are wrong," Norma said as they all returned to their jobs.

After their shift had ended Norma asked Brandt if any of his friends had been in the prisoners who had left today.

"I knew quite a few. Some were in the group who arrived here on that first train with Felix and me, but none of my barrack's mates were among them. The guys from my barracks are all busy constructing an outdoor orchestra shell to accommodate a complete orchestra of forty musicians and amphitheater seats made of bricks. The bricks are actually being made at the camp's kiln."

"I am so glad they are busy building such a special place that all the prisoners will get to enjoy. Was it your idea?" Norma asked.

"NO, but I have been helping with the work every chance I get. It will certainly enhance the sounds of the instruments." Brandt answered.

"I have not forgotten the beautiful music by Bach that I got to hear at Christmas time. Your barracks has some really great musicians and singers," Norma said.

"My friend Felix is not a musician or a singer, but he does play soccer very well and he is a good cheerleader for the musicians. I often find him watching and listening to them practice and applauding when they complete a piece."

"I have an old clarinet in my room that I played when I was in high school which seems like a hundred years ago. I can bring it to him if he would like to see if he can play it. I bet the clarinet player in the orchestra would teach him to play," Norma said.

"That is a wonderful idea. I will ask him tonight if he is interested and let you know tomorrow."

Felix did take the clarinet and began learning to play simple music, however he never was able to play most of the music that the orchestra played. Knowing that an American nurse gave the clarinet to him, gave him an appreciation for Americans that he had not had before. These new feelings helped him more easily live through the long months he remained a prisoner.

Nothing changed the established routine for many long weeks. Then one evening after Braun got back to the camp from the Fleming farm, he went looking for Brandt. He found him in the canteen and said, "I remember you saying that Rommel really was very sick when he left North Africa right before we were captured."

"Yes, that is true. Why are you thinking about that time now?" asked Brandt.

"Well, he is obviously recovered because I overheard Mr. Fleming and Mr. Bowen talking today about seeing on a newsreel that Rommel has been seen in France. They believe Hitler has sent him there to command the German forces when the Allies attempt to invade the coast of France. I don't think anyone here in the camp is aware of this happening."

"I had not heard that from anyone. If Hitler made that decision, it was very wise. I believe Rommel is the most capable man in the German army. He will attack the Allies on the beaches, not only fight defensively. If the Allies don't get a foothold in France, the war will not end successfully for many years."

"You seem to believe we still have a chance to win the war," said Braun.

"We have no chance to defeat Russia, or Great Britain at this time, but I am not sure about what will happen in Europe if the Allies don't make a successful invasion into France," Brandt said.

"I must admit we are being treated very well here in Aliceville, but I am sure ready for this war to be over and we can return home." Said Braun.

"You are still enjoying working on the Fleming farm, aren't you?" asked Brandt.

"Yes, but I do miss my mother and my sister. I have only received one letter and fear there may be problems that no one wants me to know about," answered Braun.

"Try not to worry. Living out of a city and far from any factories should be fairly safe," Brandt said. "I have only received one letter from my sister. It may be difficult to pick up letters from remote farms."

"I had not thought of that Brandt. Thank you for reminding me that Germany is more involved in the war than we are here in Aliceville," Braun said.

Brandt watched Braun walk toward his compound and remembered learning about Braun's retarded sister and knew she had to be the family member he was most worried about. He knew that life in Germany would be very difficult as the war continued. He felt sure being a prisoner of war living in the United States was a much easier life than his countrymen were experiencing.

CHAPTER 31

By the end of March over four thousand prisoners had been shipped out of Aliceville to camps outside of the state or to Alabama satellite camps. This change meant several compounds were vacant. Almost four hundred and fifty NCO's who refused to work or supervise prisoners had been segregated into one compound. Brandt told Norma these men included the last group of troublemakers left in the camp.

In order to raise the morale of the remaining prisoners, Meier requested a May Day Celebration that was quickly approved by Headquarters. Germans had been celebrating May Day to commemorate the social and economic accomplishments of the Labor movement since then end of the 1800's. Hitler had adopted this holiday for his own purposes, and the Nazis had celebrated with parades and speeches throughout Germany. The Aliceville celebration was begun with a parade of prisoners, who had worked in various industries in Germany before the war, and ended at Compound A where a tree was planted. Then all prisoners and guests were to attend a band concert. Norma and Brandt joined Felix in the audience and listened to the music together.

When the music finally ended, Norma said goodbye to Felix and Brandt started walking with her in the direction of the main gate. As soon as they were clearly separated from all the others headed away from the concert, he spoke quietly to Norma. "It is still early and I would like for us to have a few minutes for a private conversation. Come with me into the Headquarters Building. It is empty now except for the Officer of the Day who is stationed at the small office near the front door. There are plenty of areas where we can have some privacy."

"All right," Norma answered, wondering what was on Brandt's mind that had to be discussed now and in secrecy.

They entered the main door of the Headquarters Building and Brandt waved at the Officer of the Day who saw them and was about to rise up from his desk when his phone rang and he just waved back at Brandt and reached for the phone. Brandt took Norma's arm and hurried her down the hall and into an office where there were several chairs and a small sofa away from the desk and filing cabinet.

"The last time I was here, I saw this office and hoped it wouldn't be locked. Make yourself comfortable on this sofa and we can have a few minutes to talk," Brandt said as he sat down in the chair closest to where Norma was seated.

"Is there a problem at the hospital that is worrying you?" she asked.

"Absolutely not. I just wanted some time alone with you," he answered.

"This is certainly nicer than a back hall in the hospital with all the noise and smell of antiseptic," she said.

"Norma, there are several things I want to say, need to say, to you. I don't want to delay saying them because with the number of prisoners being reduced almost daily, I have realized I might be sent away at any time. You probably have not heard that Karl Braun was notified that he is leaving tomorrow to go to the branch camp at Greenville, Alabama where he will work in the lumber and wood products industries. I am not sure if or when he will return to Aliceville," Brandt began talking.

"No, I did not know that. If Mr. Bowen was called, he had not called my dad before I left home."

"I am sure your parents will be notified by the time you get home tonight."

"I am really disappointed that Braun is moving. He has been a great help to Mr. Bowen. He is not as old as my dad, but he is definitely too old to run the farm without help. Every time I visit the farm I realize he has given more work to Braun," Norma said.

"I will be coming here to Headquarters in the morning and one of my requests will be to let me work at your farm until I leave," Brandt said.

"I know that the number of patients has dropped dramatically these past weeks with the camp numbers dropping so significantly, but you would be the last orderly anyone would release from the hospital. You know how all the doctors, even the German doctors, treasure you," Norma said.

"That will change after I speak to the Commander tomorrow. Now wait until I explain why that is true before you disagree with me," Brandt hurriedly spoke up.

Norma was prepared to speak up, but on hearing Brandt's plea she held her tongue. She did have a questioning look in her eyes as she stared at him.

"I know my words are going to shock you, but please don't stop listening until you have heard the whole story. It is a long story with many twists and turns. I will start by saying my name is not Victor Brandt. My name is actually Dirk Wagner. I am actually Doctor Dirk Wagner. I graduated from King's College London with a medical degree in 1935. I am one hundred percent German but my mother had a cousin who married an English Lord and my family visited in England many times before the Great War. When Germany got bogged down in that earlier war, my mother insisted I go to England to complete my medical training which I had begun at Heidelberg University. When I returned to Germany, I began my practice in surgery at several hospitals in Berlin.

Although many German doctors were more politically minded than I, I never joined the Nazi Party. My mother was a friend of Rommel's mother and those two ladies both were concerned that my failure to become a Nazi could lead to my being ostracized or imprisoned and I was asked to join the Army. I did and was placed on Rommel's staff just before he was sent to North Africa as the Commander of the German forces there.

When Rommel became ill and was ordered to leave, I asked to be placed in a field hospital where I felt my skills as a surgeon could best be used. I worked there for several months and on one rare day when I was not operating, I offered to help carry wounded soldiers on stretchers into the hospital. I soon realized that we were losing ground on the battlefield, and my heart was broken for these very young men who were dying in unusually high numbers. When the stretcher bearer I was helping was suddenly killed and his body was lying next to me, I decided to change places with him. I exchanged our shirts and identification. A few minutes later when I was captured, I was believed to be a recruit in the Army and not an officer. My decision allowed me to be a mentor to many of these young men and prevented them from actions that could have resulted in death, anxiety, depression, and other destructive behaviors. I know one soldier in particular who I convinced not to commit suicide. Norma, I had no idea until I arrived here at Aliceville that I would have the opportunity to actually work in an American hospital where I could care for my fellow prisoners and American military patients as well. I also had no idea that I would meet the most beautiful lady I had ever seen and would fall in love with her. Norma, your beauty is stunning, but I also fell in love with an angelic nurse who cares about relieving pain in an expert and timely way. Finally, I believe you love me as well."

Norma had sat spellbound listening to Brandt. When he stopped talking, she didn't speak for almost a minute.

"I know I have given you a great deal to process, but I am waiting for you to react to me," Brandt spoke anxiously.

"I am in total shock. Please give me some time to consider all that you have just told me. I know my feelings for you have grown from the first day when I saw a very attractive man coming toward me. I have complete faith in my love for you, but I thought we could never have a future together. Please take me to the gate now. I will talk to you tomorrow."

CHAPTER 32

Norma had not set an alarm last night because her thoughts had been swirling with Brandt's confession. She awakened at the same time she usually did anyway. When she finally made her way downstairs, her father had already left. "Did Dad call Milton before he went to work?" she asked Florence.

"No, but I expect he will call him from the store. I know he will be disappointed that Braun is not going to get out of the doghouse and be able to return to work."

"Brandt may be in the doghouse today. Oh, I shouldn't have said that. Please forget I said it," said Norma.

"Why do you think Brandt is in trouble?" Florence asked.

"Mother, I said please forget I said that. When he is not in the hospital working, he is all over the camp helping everyone," Norma answered. "He doesn't hesitate to go to headquarters or Sgt. Meier about anything he sees or hears that seems to have a potential problem for the prisoners or the Americans."

"I certainly know he has become your friend. You rarely mention the camp or your job there without mentioning him," said Florence.

"I didn't realize that I talked about him so much. He has become a friend," Norma answered. "How about a cup of coffee?" she asked trying to change the subject.

"I also have gravy and biscuits," Florence said as she brought Norma a plate and sat down at the table with her daughter.

Norma was very careful to keep their conversation on the food or the house the rest of the time she spent with her mother that morning. When it got late enough that she could head to work without being questioned as to why she was going early, she changed into her nurse's uniform and left the house. All the way to the prison camp, she anticipated what she would learn about Brandt's meeting with the commander.

As she passed through the gates to enter the camp, she saw nothing out of order. The final guard she passed was actually yawning. "Sorry," he said. "I stayed up too late last night playing cards."

"Nothing is happening very exciting today it seems," Norma replied.

The guard just nodded and Norma walked toward the hospital. When she approached the door Brandt appeared and said, "I need to talk to you before you go to work."

She followed him in the direction of the Headquarters. They both finally stopped walking and Brandt turned to her. "I have been with the commander all morning and need to bring you up to date. I told him all about what I did in North Africa and the reasons I did it. I also told him that I had been to the U.S. several times at Harvard Medical School, Mass General Hospital and John Hopkins teaching about a specific way I had changed and improved several surgical procedures. I know I didn't tell you that, but I told him before I requested that he contact each of those places to verify what I told him and ask if either one would allow me to join their staff."

"What is he going to do?" Norma asked.

"He had my picture taken and he is going to send it to his superiors in Washington D.C. along with the information I told him. It will be up to the ranking officers at Army Headquarters in Washington to decide about my request. This will all take some time. I am not sure how long. The commander immediately decided that I can no longer work in the hospital here. He even told me to continue being Victor Brandt until there is official notification from Washington that I am Dirk Wagner."

"Oh, what a relief. I was worried that he would laugh at you or be mad and put you in lockdown," Norma said.

I was very respectful of him and his position and thankfully he is very intelligent and has interviewed other German officers. I was able to convince him that I am who I say I am."

"Do you expect to be sent to Harvard or one of those other places right now while the war is continuing?" Norma asked.

"I would like to think that is the case. We have German doctors working here who don't wear the prison uniform I am currently wearing and even walk into town at their leisure."

"I have accepted my first love was over and I was free to follow my heart. I know, and you know that I fell in love with you. I am still adjusting to this new situation. Remember, just two days ago I had no idea that you were a prestigious doctor who had taught at Harvard," Norma said.

"Since I can no longer work in the hospital here, please think about asking for me to be allowed to work at the farm where Braun has been working. I really want to meet your family and friends and may not know as much as Braun knew about farming, but you could teach me," Brandt said.

"I hadn't thought of that until you just brought it up. I will certainly make that suggestion; however, I do not want to tell my parents about who you really are until it has been verified and you are recognized by the camp," Norma said.

"I think that is an excellent idea. I know your brother is in England awaiting the invasion into Europe. At this time your parents are not truly interested in knowing that we have fallen in love," Brandt said.

"Thank you for understanding how delicate this situation may become," Norma admitted. Just remember that I am in love with you!"

"I do understand. I am confident we will be able to work something out eventually," Brandt said.

"I am going to feel very foolish giving you orders about patients now," Norma admitted.

"Haven't I always acted appropriately? Besides, you have never asked me to do anything that was dangerous for the patient," he answered.

"Thank you for that, but I notice you said, 'dangerous' not unnecessary or useless."

"I know that sometimes you were just following the doctor's orders and didn't expect you to tell an orderly what you thought about the orders. Some of the doctors here have really impressed me with their knowledge," he answered.

"Yes, well, I will acknowledge I have more respect for some than I have for others."

"Overall, the hospital here has the newest equipment, medicines, and facilities that I have witnessed, and a staff equal to any I have seen. I think I have kept up with what is happening in medicine during my time here. I also found out that my surgery skills have not deserted me when I had to do that emergency surgery," Dirk said.

"That is high praise coming from the extinguished Dr. Dirk Wagner for The Aliceville Internment Camp Hospital," Norma said.

"Well, I should have included the nursing staff that is here as well," he quickly added.

"Thank you for those kind words," Norma added. After a quick embrace they both smiled at each other and Norma headed to the hospital and Dirk headed back to his barracks.

CHAPTER 33

In a couple of days Brandt was working at the Fleming farm. Norma came to the farm every time she could leave her parents. She and Brandt rode horses all over the farm and watched the seedlings growing into cotton, corn, carrots, eggplant, lettuce, cucumbers and tomatoes. The Bowens often invited Norma and her parents for meals and Norma would contact the camp to report Brandt would be returning late for a myriad of reasons from aiding a veterinarian with a difficult birth of an animal, to the truck breaking down, and even to Milton falling off a ladder!

Brandt became more comfortable with the Bowens and Flemings every time they were all together for meals. It happened that the Normandy Invasion was announced on the radio one evening when Brandt was sitting at the table with both couples and Norma. George immediately led the group in a prayer where he prayed for this invasion to lead to a quick end of the war and for the safety of his son Ben. Everyone noted that Brandt bowed his head and joined the entire group in pronouncing "Amen."

That particular evening Norma drove Brandt back to the prison camp. "I needed to drive you back tonight. I know hearing about the large number of casualties must have reminded you of North Africa. Rommel is your friend, I know."

"Yes, we were friends from my boyhood. He will do all he can to prevent this invasion from being successful, but I doubt he will be successful in the end. Tonight that battlefield is a killing field. Norma. I was not offended by your father's prayer. I certainly join him in praying for your brother's safety."

"Thank you. I am not sure who will be here to pick you up in the morning, but one of us will be here. I know you haven't heard from Washington yet, and I know that waiting to hear is very hard."

"It has given me this opportunity to meet your family and friends, especially Larry and Connie Gardner, and gave them an opportunity to get to know at least one German personally. I know this can only have a positive effect on our future. I am very sorry that you will not get an opportunity to meet my family."

"I am so sorry that both of your parents are dead. I know they were so proud when you finished medical school. If you had chosen another career, we may have never met."

"That is true I guess, but I believe it only took the chance that I would see you for me to fall in love. I will always remember that first time I saw you walking across the floor in the hospital to meet me and my heart doing a flip in my chest," he said.

Norma laughed and said, "I remember that day. I met a tall, blond man with sky blue eyes smiling at me."

"Yes, but you didn't smile back. You were all business!"

"I knew I had to be. In my mind, it was up to me to keep us busy doing our jobs."

"I'm so glad I was able to finally move us beyond that first day."

They both got out of the car and embraced in a loving moment with a passionate kiss before they separated and he almost ran to the gate instead of what he wanted to do.

"Goodnight, Dirk," she quietly said to herself as she got back into the car and drove to her home.

It was actually one week later that Norma got a call from Headquarters asking her to come to Col. Waite's office before she reported to the hospital. She hurriedly dressed and left the house calling to her mother as she left, "Sorry Mom, I have to report to work early today. Don't worry, no crisis!"

Norma walked into Col. Waite's office in less than an hour since she had received the call. She said, "Good morning, I am Norma Fleming and I received a call to report here before I go to work."

"Go right in. He Is expecting you," said the secretary.

When she entered his office door, the Col. rose from his desk and came to shake her hand. "Thank you for coming so promptly. I have been asked to call you by Dr. Dirk Wagner."

Norma looked shocked and didn't know what to say.

"Don't be upset Norma. Please be seated and let me bring you up to date on Dr. Wagner's status."

Once Norma was seated, the secretary entered with coffee for Norma and the Col. Norma wasn't sure she could hold the cup without her hand shaking so she didn't dare pick up the cup.

"I received word last evening that Dr. Wagner's identification had been confirmed at Harvard Medical School and he was to report to the Dept. of the Army in Washington as soon as possible. He was picked up by helicopter at daybreak and was taken to Birmingham where he will get a train to Washington. He asked me to tell you that he will notify you where he is as soon as he is settled. Do you have any questions?"

"I am trying to process all you have just told me. I really don't have any questions now, but I hope you will keep me informed if I don't hear from him within a short time. I know you have many responsibilities, and I certainly don't want to be an irritant, but I do appreciate your taking time to tell me about Dirk," Norma said.

"Nurse Fleming, I have enjoyed this opportunity to meet you and share our interest in Dr. Wagner. You may not know that I have known him since I first arrived here at Aliceville Internment Camp as Col. Prince's replacement. He was extremely helpful in identifying the Nazi prisoners who were attacking the others often quite violently."

".He told me about how he convinced the Germans in North Africa that he was Victor Brandt, a stretcher bearer, in order to not be identified as an officer after he was captured. He recognized that he wanted to be with the soldiers so he could help them adjust to being prisoners. I know of specific cases where he prevented suicide and escape attempts. For over a year he had me convinced he was an orderly as we worked together caring for both prisoners and Americans who were patients in the hospital," Norma said.

"He is obviously a very intelligent man who is more concerned for others than his own personal safety," Col. Waite stated. "Both of us will have to standby now and see what his future holds."

"Please pray it includes me," Norma said as she rose and left the Col.'s office.

CHAPTER 34

The Webb Photography business had continued to excel. It had been so successful that for Christmas 1943 the owners had given themselves a large sailing vessel. There were two berths, a small kitchen and a sitting area below the main deck. Every weekend that winter that the weather permitted they went aboard Friday night and sat sail at daybreak Saturday morning and only arrived back after dark on Sunday evening. When the schools in Panama City were not in session for Easter Break 1944, the Webbs sailed to Tampa to observe McDill Field.

James and John sailed from the Gulf into Tampa Bay passing St. Petersburg and got as close to the base as they could without drawing attention to themselves and took pictures of the airplanes flying in and out of the base. They knew MacDill Field was the home base of the planes searching for German subs in the Gulf of Mexico. It also functioned as a stop on the ferrying of planes from the U.S. to the Pacific. They knew their Germans operators needed that knowledge also.

After five days living on the sailboat, the Webbs were ready for good showers and different food, so they sailed south in the bay in search of a marina where they could stay for a few days. They found one on the north side of St. Petersburg and dropped their anchor. They used their dingy to paddle ashore and found they were at a resort and checked into a room facing the water where they could actually see their sailboat. That night in the resort dining room they carried out their usual routine of finding locals to talk with and found out more details about MacDill that they would add to the pictures when the information was passed on to their contact in New Orleans.

On the trip back to Panama City, they enjoyed sailing and discussed the gasoline rations they had not used! "It certainly took us much longer to get all the way to Tampa, but think about the gas we didn't burn," said James.

"I know. We have to save as much as possible before we make the trip to Fort Benning, Georgia. It is one of the largest army posts in the States, and I have had it on our list of places we must visit since we arrived," John added.

"What exactly do we know, or I mean, what do you know about Fort Benning?"

"I know the Army has its Officer Candidate School there for one thing. One of our customers when we first opened the shop wanted to send her brother a picture of his dog that she was keeping for him while he was in the Officer Candidate School at Ft. Benning," John said.

"Oh yea, I remember passing that customer on to you while I took on that crying baby," James answered. "I was too busy trying to entertain that kid to ask about the dog."

"I remember it was a black Labrador Retriever named Samson. He was a great dog that did exactly what he was told. I understood why that man wanted to make sure his dog would be treated well while he was away in the army," said John.

"That was a beautiful girl bringing him to have his picture taken. I believe you enjoyed talking to her more than taking the dog's picture," said James.

"She was easy to talk to and told me all about her brother and where he was and why she had his dog," John explained.

"Wish I had taken the dog and given you the crying baby," said James.

"We have about run out of places to photograph. Do you think we should consider leaving here and heading home?"

The two men stared at each other for a long moment. Finally, both spoke at once. "Not now!" said one, "No way!" the other.

"We have a thriving business here and after the war it should grow even more."

"I agree, John. Our business has been very successful here. Probably more successful than in Germany, but we will have to just wait and see how the post-war era treats us."

"I don't believe the newspapers here are telling the real story of the war. That Normandy Invasion is a made-up story I believe. Rommel was in France with our forces, and I feel sure he sent them back to Great Britain licking their wounds."

"On our next trip to New Orleans maybe our contact will have a real German newspaper and we can really learn how the war is going."

These two German spies had convinced themselves that the war was progressing and the fatherland was actually winning the war. No other scenario seemed possible for them, but they had really enjoyed living in the states and were somehow hoping for a German victory, with them left living in the U.S.

They never spoke of Aliceville and the German prisoners who didn't want their help in escaping. They believed those prisoners had been tortured and were afraid of being shot at any moment. However, they always kept enough stolen gas ration cards to get to New Orleans with the belief that they could get into Mexico and head for Argentina where there was a steady group of Nazi sympathizers awaiting a ship or submarine to take them back to the safety of Europe.

During the following months, the two men had to finally accept that the Axis Powers were actually being defeated when the American newspapers were reporting the advances that the Americans were making and all the people they had dinner with each evening were talking of the coming defeat of Germany. When they heard one man talking about German prisoners pouring into the states again and the Aliceville camp being back to full capacity, they knew it was time to leave.

"I certainly didn't expect that we would actually ever find ourselves in this situation. I really believed that Normandy invasion would be where we began winning. Now, I believe we will have to figure how to close our business and clear out," said John.

"I think we have successfully convinced the people we have met here in Panama City that we are Americans, but the idea of never being able to return to Germany and visit our families is not acceptable," said James.

They had paid for the lease of the house where the shop was located through 1945 so they knew they had time to get away. They sold as much as possible of their equipment and furniture in the first months of 1945 and then packed the two best cameras and their clothes. They withdrew their money from the bank and told the teller they were returning to New Jersey. Then they headed to New Orleans. They parked their car on a back street where crime was common. They left the car windows open and the keys in the ignition knowing that after a day or so someone could easily get in and drive it away.

Their contact met them at their usual meeting place and they explained that this time they were going to pay him to not only take pictures, but also take them all the way to Argentina. The contact named a high price expecting them to argue, but was surprised when James pulled out the money from his wallet and handed it to the contact. The contact accepted the money and accompanied both men into Mexico where in a remote area he shot them both in the back, stole their money, clothes and cameras, and dumped their dead bodies into the Gulf of Mexico before he headed to Argentina himself.

CHAPTER 35

Dirk Wagner had arrived in Washington D.C. and was immediately taken to the Army Department where he was interviewed about his time at the Aliceville Prison Camp and even the surgery he had done on the German prisoner. It was obvious that Col. Waite had made a complete report on him. He was surprised to learn that the Americans already knew that he had been on Rommel's staff in North Africa, but thought he had been killed during the fighting. Following his explanation of the day when he had assumed Victor Brandt's identity, he was taken to Walter Reed Military Hospital where he was assigned to the chief of surgery. Within twenty-four hours he was operating on wounded Americans soldiers and sailors and wounded German prisoners who were arriving hourly. He was given a nice room and ate with the doctors in their private dining room. Appropriate clothes were issued to him and of course the white coat of a doctor. His only duty besides surgery was to speak German to any prisoner who was terrified of torture or medical experiments similar to the ones done in Germany.

It was several weeks before he had an afternoon when he had the time to write Norma the following letter.

Dearest Norma,

I know Col. Waite told you that a helicopter picked me up and took me to the train in Birmingham that left for Washington immediately after I boarded. Here I was interviewed at Army Headquarters and then assigned to Walter Reed Military Hospital where I was put to work doing surgery on seriously wounded Americans and Germans. I rarely have any time off except to sleep. I have no idea when I will be sent to Harvard or any of the hospitals where there are doctors who vouched for me. It is possible that I will be sent back to Germany after the war before I get to come to Aliceville. Please know that I love you dearly, and want to spend the rest of my life as your husband. I will write you as often as possible, but I am not sure I will receive any letters you write to Walter Reed for me. Please try anyway. Do remember all of our letters could be read by the sensors.

With all my love, Dirk

Norma returned a letter to Dirk that afternoon.

Dearest Dirk,

I was so thrilled when I got your letter. I wish I could come to Washington to hopefully see you. However, you know I must stay here with my parents at least until my brother returns home. My parents' health continues to decline. Thankfully my father can still walk to the hardware store, but mother's eyes are getting so bad she cannot cook a meal without my help. New hospital workers have been among our growing prison population so the hospital continues to adequately treat all wounded and sick personal at the camp. My hours have not increased as of now, but I would not be surprised if I am asked to at least work some weekends.

I cannot express how much I miss our working together and the few stolen times we have spent together. Please get as much rest as possible and know that I am praying for the end of the war and a bright future for us.

I love and miss you every moment,

Norma

Dirk and Norma exchanged letters over the next months, but it was in October 1944 that Dirk wrote the letter to Norma where he finally expressed his anger with Hitler, his disappointment with his native country, and his lack of ever wanting to return to Germany.

Dear Norma,

I probably should not be writing this letter until I have had time to get over the anger that I am currently experiencing. I know that you will have heard by the time you get this letter that Field Marshall Ervin Rommel is dead. I know he was at the meeting held in July where there was an attempt to assassinate Hitler. Although it was reported that Rommel died from injuries he received when his staff car was strafed by a Canadian Spitfire in Normandy, I know that is untrue. Several German prisoners I have met here have told me all of the officers Hitler believed had planned the assassination are being executed. Hitler's paranoia is obviously out of control. It is obvious that Germany has lost this war and instead of accepting that he must admit this defeat, he is asking for the entire country to be burned. My God, he appears to have no love for his country and no honor.

Norma, there are many beautiful places in Germany that I had hoped to show you, but that may not happen. Right now, I am so disappointed in the influence of the Nazi Party and Hitler that I hope to remain here in the United States with you. Days like today I really miss seeing your beautiful face and holding you in my arms.

Love, Dirk

Norma decided to wait until the next day to answer this letter and give herself time to think about how to best answer. When she arrived at the hospital the following day, she knew she had made the right decision because the prisoners had already asked to be allowed to have a memorial ceremony for the Field Marshal and it had been approved. Norma wrote that she heard many American staff members express admiration for his intelligence and military capabilities. When the service was held on October 25, 1944, Norma wrote about every event and speech that was given. She described in detail the large portrait of Rommel that one of the prisoners had painted that was on display on the platform showing the Desert Fox with all of his war decorations on full display on his uniform. She listed the American officers that Dirk would know by name who attended, and her family along with a group of Aliceville citizens who also attended. Two chaplains offered prayers and all present joined in the Lord's Prayer in German and English. The service ended with the orchestra playing and the prisoners all singing "Once I Had a Comrade" that Norma knew Dirk would have expected to be sung as it was always sung at German military funerals.

Over the following months Dirk and Norma exchanged letters almost daily. Dirk wrote about the war that he heard about daily, and Norma wrote about her family and the farm. Dirk occasionally wrote about a patient who had told him about the current conditions in Germany, but Norma rarely mentioned the prison camp. She knew that Dirk knew only a very few of the current prisoners and would be distressed by lockdowns, bread and water punishments, silly antics like flying balloons over the prison walls and raining small black painted swastikas on Aliceville! Yet all of their letters included their love and commitment to each other.

CHAPTER 36

World War II finally ended in Europe when the Germans surrendered to the Allies on May 8, 1945. Celebrations broke out in every city and town in the U.S. Norma and her family and friends in Aliceville joined in by raising flags, singing in the streets, and thanking God. Most of the people in Aliceville expected the prisoners housed there would be leaving soon to return to Germany to rebuild their lives.

However, that was not what happened. As the Americans learned about the concentration camps where Jews had been exterminated and the foul treatment and starvation Allied prisoners had received throughout Germany, sympathy for Germany was gone. The Geneva Convention was no longer the law of the land. Food became limited and opportunities for prisoners disappeared. Norma only received one final letter from Dirk written from Washington D.C. He wrote that he had been told to pack his few belongings and be prepared to leave. She wrote back, but no answer came from Dirk. A friend he had made with an American doctor at Walter Reed finally wrote her that Dirk had been sent to Great Britian.

Norma felt like she would soon get a letter from him because she knew he had attended medical school in London and surely still had friends there. Weeks passed and no letter came from Dirk. Norma continued working at the camp hospital and watched the prisoners being moved out. Japan surrendered September 15, 1945. Camp Aliceville was officially closed on September 30, 1945 and Norma's brother returned from England as a civilian. Still no letter came from Dirk.

Norma had been thinking of where she would go now that the war had ended, her brother was back and Dirk had disappeared. Even though the prison was being dismantled, Aliceville remained filled with memories, and she knew she could no longer remain there. As she sat on her parents' front porch one afternoon, the postman walked up to the mailbox and on seeing her walked to the porch and handed her a letter. It was a letter from Dirk Wagner. She felt her hand shaking as she opened the letter she had been waiting for so long!

Dirk wrote that he had thought that he was leaving the U.S. to go to England, but he explained his paperwork was somehow lost and he ended up in a postwar prison brigade in France. He explained that his location was typical of many brigades scattered throughout the countries that had been damaged by the Germans in the war, and German prisoners were being used to rebuild cities, factories and bridges. He wrote that he was fluent in French and could translate for the Germans who could not speak or read French. He had no idea when he might be released., but expected to be held indefinitely. He admitted that his speaking French allowed him to be able to bribe one of his guards to mail her this one letter, but Norma realized that she should expect no more. She was very aware that Dirk made no reference to any future plans.

The next week Norma left Aliceville and moved to Birmingham, Alabama. Her parents understood her need to get away. She had no trouble getting a job at Hilman Hospital and requested the night shift. For the next two years, she was heartbroken and chose to work nights and weekends. Men often asked her out, but she politely declined. She realized that her heart still belonged to Dirk. She wondered if she would ever get past the hurt and be able to marry and have a family.

One morning she left the hospital and headed to her car. Suddenly she looked up and saw a man that looked like Dirk leaning on the front door of the car. She took a moment to realize that it was indeed Dirk and she saw the same smile and big blue eyes she had seen all those years ago on the first day she met him in the Camp Aliceville Hospital.

She began to slowly walk towards him. He reached out his arms to her and she moved into them. He tilted up her head and said, "How are you?" She replied, "Much better now, what happened? Why didn't you write? How did you know where I was?"

He responded, "I went to Aliceville and saw your parents and asked about you. Your parents asked me those same questions and, in the beginning, they did not want to tell me where you were. I assured them that I had not come back to just upend your life. I told them that I had been in brigades to help rebuild Europe and did not have a way to contact anyone because we were moved all of the time and would never be able to get a return letter. I told them that I loved you and that I had come back to explain what had happened. I hoped, but had no reason to believe, that you had not moved on with your life.

They then told me that you had not dated or married anyone. I told them that I was back to work in the United States having finally been released from the brigades. I reached out to a friend of mine who is a doctor that I knew from Harvard and asked him to help me get a work permit and job as a doctor in the United States. He got me an interview and I have a job now at Massachusetts General Hospital. They offered me a job last week and I will begin work the first of the month.

I told your parents that I had no right to expect you to have waited for me, but that I was coming to see you and to ask you to marry me. Your parents gave me their blessing if I could convince you. They told me where you were and your work schedule. I drove in this morning and was waiting for you. I love you and have thought of you every day. I have a week before I have to be at work and wanted to ask you for a date!"

She tilted her head up and looked at him. "I thought you told me that you told my parents you wanted to marry me." He looked deeply into her eyes and said, "I do, but we have not even had a real date."

She smiled and said, "I am free for breakfast!"

He smiled and reached his hand into his pocket, took out a diamond engagement ring, bent down on one knee in the parking lot, and said, "Will you marry me if the date goes well?"

She grinned and took that ring. It was beautiful and tears came to her eyes as she said, "Yes, to the marriage if the date goes well."

He stood up and wrapped her in his arms. He bent his head to kiss her. "Let's go to breakfast and plan the rest of our lives together."

Finally, for Norma and Dirk there was a bright future and it happened in Aliceville.

THE END

ABOUT THE AUTHOR

J.F. Brindley, an accomplished educator and author, holds degrees from the University of Vermont and the University of Oklahoma. With a rich career spanning 20 years, she has taught in Virginia and the Panama Canal Zone, and served as a high school administrator in Florida. Post-retirement, Brindley found her passion in writing, creating engaging stories for both adults and children. Her previous work includes the delightful tales of *The Wacky Witch* and *A Bunny Rabbit Named Cloud* in addition to The Mallory Mystery Series including *Journey of the Jewelry, Not all of the Answers,* and *Darling Emily.* Now, she brings her unique storytelling to *It Happened in Aliceville,* promising another captivating read. Her biography is a testament to her dedication to education and literature.

Milton Keynes UK
Ingram Content Group UK Ltd.
UKHW021931130824
446844UK00012B/837